The Murail siblings are [...] their own right – Marie-Aude has sold over two million books worldwide, Elvire's very first novel was turned into a film and Lorris is well known for writing about his two passions: good food and science fiction. Together they make a truly formidable literary trio. When writing the Golem series, the siblings wanted not only to recapture the intensity and creativity of playing together as children, but also to write the kinds of books they would have liked when they were young. "It was like a game," says Elvire, the youngest. "It was a huge challenge, but we wanted to lose our individual voices and morph into a new, even better one. It worked so well that sometimes we had trouble remembering who had written what!" Her sister Marie-Aude adds, "It's so important to remember what you were like when you were young. It gets more difficult as you get older – you have to have your own children to get it back again!" It took two years to complete all five Golem books.

Now it is your turn to play...

GOLEM

This book is supported by the French
Ministry for Foreign Affairs, as part of
the Burgess programme headed for
the French Embassy in London by the
Institut Français du Royaume-Uni

Liberté • Égalité • Fraternité
RÉPUBLIQUE FRANÇAISE

Golem
3: Natasha

Elvire, Lorris and Marie-Aude Murail
translated by Sarah Adams

WALKER BOOKS
AND SUBSIDIARIES
LONDON • BOSTON • SYDNEY • AUCKLAND

First published 2005 by Walker Books Ltd
87 Vauxhall Walk, London SE11 5HJ

2 4 6 8 10 9 7 5 3 1

Original Edition: *Golem 3 – Natacha*
© 2002 Éditions Pocket Jeunesse,
division of Univers Poche, Paris – France
Translation © 2005 Sarah Adams
Cover image © 2005 Guy McKinley

The right of Elvire, Lorris and Marie-Aude Murail to be
identified as authors of this work has been asserted by them
in accordance with the Copyright, Designs and Patents Act 1988

This book has been typeset in DeadHistory and M Joanna

Printed and bound in Great Britain
by Bookmarque Ltd, Croydon, Surrey

British Library Cataloguing in Publication Data:
a catalogue record for this book
is available from the British Library

ISBN 1-84428-616-9

www.walkerbooks.co.uk

Contents

In Golem: LEVEL 2:

Something is haunting the basements of Hummingbird Tower. And it looks a lot like the golem in the pirate game that's hijacking everybody's computers. Majid has received several visits from people keen to get their hands on his prize computer — two "delivery men" from Price Shrinkers, and Albert, a scruffy man who claims he invented Golem. A craze has started for Big B farting goo (especially the scented and fluorescent combos), even the grown-ups are collecting it. And now Natasha and Bubble, two more characters from the Golem game, have escaped into teacher Hugh's bedroom — and the real world...

0%
10%
20%
30%
40%
50%
60
70%
80
90

...100%

››Transfer complete

START PLAY ››

Let's Not Talk About It

There aren't many people who can keep a secret.
And when it's a monstrous secret, you need to be
particularly strong-minded. Hugh and his mother
were both keeping a monstrous secret, because they
didn't want to frighten each other.

Mrs Mullins had seen some sort of flying lizard
or miniature dragon in her son's study. It had tumbled out of a sleeve when she was folding a shirt.
Of course, there was nothing to stop her saying to
Hugh, "Guess what? While you were out, I saw a
little dragon in your study."

But somehow she couldn't see herself doing it.
Being a psychologist, she'd only ever given her son

sensible advice. Perhaps she could make a confession. "Guess what? I've gone mad. I keep seeing strange creatures crawling out of your shirts."

But Hugh would only say, "You should take it easy, Mum."

Mrs Mullins played and replayed the scene in her head, adding a sentence here, cutting one there. Should she blame the farting goo? After all, hadn't they said on TV there were rumours of a hallucinogenic FG? And hadn't she handled the FG tubs she'd found in Hugh's study when she was prising the lids off? Was that enough to trigger a hallucination? She was clutching at straws. But as night fell, she had another idea: maybe the little dragon really did exist. At least that would account for the holes in her carpet, not to mention the odd smell.

"Don't you think there's an odd smell?" she asked at supper.

Hugh spluttered. Nothing seemed odd right now. There was a monster in the basements of Hummingbird Tower that gave you electric shocks and talked drivel. Not only that, but the monster looked like Joke, the blob-shaped golem from his computer game. If he'd been the only one who'd seen it, he would have told himself, You've gone stir-fry crazy. But there'd been three other witnesses: Sebastian, Samir and Lulu.

"No, it smells delicious," he murmured distractedly, sniffing his soup and dunking his fork in his bowl.

"It's easier with a spoon," said his mother.

They both laughed nervously. Hugh opened his mouth. He *had* to tell her what was going on. He couldn't carry on like this.

"Mum..."

"Yes?"

They stared at each other. Here we go, thought Mrs Mullins, he's noticed I'm going mad.

"What kind of soup is it?" asked Hugh.

"It's got carrots, potatoes, turnips," his mother recited, her voice close to breaking.

Something inside Hugh snapped. Too bad, he thought. I'm going to tell her everything. I saw a golem, I'll say. There's a golem in the basements of Hummingbird Tower. "There's a... Are there any leeks in it?"

"Don't you like them?" she asked timidly. "You've never liked lizards very much."

"*What?*"

Mrs Mullins turned pale. "Did I ... did I just say something ludicrous?"

"You mentioned lizards."

"No, I said *ludicrous*."

"*Ludicrous?* Weird!"

They both laughed shakily. Keeping their secrets was driving them mad.

"I'm going to visit my sister in Sunny-on-Sea," Mrs Mullins suddenly announced.

"When?"

"Tomorrow. I need a rest. Yes. A rest will do me good." There were tears in her eyes. She was deserting him. Abandoning her son to the claws of a dragon. Just as well it was only twenty centimetres tall.

"But ... will you be away long?"

"Probably a week. Will you be all right without me?"

Hugh nodded. But he knew he'd never survive on his own in the flat, with only a computer that switched itself on for company. He had to talk to somebody. Majid? Samir? Sebastian? They were just kids.

"Albert," he whispered.

"What?" asked his mother.

They looked at each other. They were on the verge of blurting everything out, but they just couldn't do it.

"I've … I've got to do some reading for an evening class. It's about Albert," stammered Hugh. "Albert Einstein."

He got up from the table, even though he'd hardly touched his soup. Yes, that was it, he needed to speak to Albert, the fugitive who claimed to have invented Golem.

"But where is he?" he wondered, half to himself and half out loud.

"In your study," answered Mrs Mullins.

"What?"

"There's a B Smart book on Einstein in your study." Atomic bombs and dragons. She mopped her brow. "I'm going to bed."

Alone in his study, Hugh glanced fearfully at his electric blue computer. After clearing out his wallet, Albert had said, "If I need to get hold of you, I'll email."

Maybe he had. But Hugh didn't dare click on the Outlook Express icon to pick up his messages. He stroked the mouse softly. The screen quivered and an image popped up. His favourite.

"Well, *hello* there!"

Natasha was in flirt mode, her hands resting coyly on her hips. Hugh traced the girl-golem's outline with his finger: her mouth, her breasts, her bare thighs. He blinked. He could hardly see her for tears.

"Well, *hello* there!" she repeated.

"Oh, be quiet." Hugh flopped into his chair, reached over to the printer and grabbed the piece of paper there.

Play with me. I'm waiting for you!

His mother claimed the printer had started working of its own accord. Mrs Mullins muddled up faxes and emails, so she hadn't been particularly alarmed. But Hugh knew that messages didn't spontaneously appear from an ordinary printer. It was even signed.

Natasha

Had Albert invented a game whose characters could interact with the real world? It was ridiculous. Unthinkable. But Joke was in the basements of Hummingbird Tower right now, blowing all the fuses to satisfy his appetite for electricity. It was ridiculous. Impossible!

"Ridiculous," Hugh whispered, eyes glued to Natasha. A crazy idea was forming. If Joke had escaped from the game, why couldn't Natasha? He caressed the flat image with the back of his hand. She was his adolescent dream, the girl who'd haunted his fantasies at a time when his friends had teased him for being a wimp.

Natasha's curves were designed to make super-models green with envy. She was wasp-waisted, her eyes were somewhere between gold and emerald, and her mouth looked like it was always being kissed. With her she-warrior's frame, pneumatic breasts and eraser-laser slung over her shoulder, she could seduce anybody and kill anybody too. But her creator had failed in one thing: when Hugh clicked on *obedient* for her character, he'd got stuck with *aggressive*. Albert hadn't had time to fine-tune certain details and, worse still, he hadn't had time to finish off the game. What was the point of playing with the girl-golem if she couldn't gain a soul from the Master Golem at the end of her quest?

But Hugh's fondness for Natasha eventually conquered his fear, and he gave the mouse a nudge. "Are you in an aggressive mood?" he asked.

The image jumped. Natasha seized her weapon and aimed it at the outside world. Directly at Hugh. Instinctively he swivelled back in his chair.

"Calm down!"

But she had already turned her back on him and was heading off down an unknown path. Hugh had never seen this part of the game before. Had Albert lied? Had he led Natasha to the Master Golem after all? The girl-golem was striding confidently along under a magnificently starry sky.

One of the stars started flashing, then grew bigger. Bigger and bigger. Hugh blinked. It had filled the screen and was twinkling from all five points, as brightly as the star above the manger in Bethlehem. There was a little square in each point. By now, Hugh was familiar with the rattling sound of an old typewriter that came through the speakers. The following words appeared on the screen:

I am that which is known by another name.

Hugh whispered the riddle. He moved the cursor and clicked randomly on the little empty boxes. They flashed in turn, but nothing happened.

"*That which is known by another name?*" he wondered out loud.

He was hooked. He'd forgotten all about the nightmare earlier this afternoon. Once again, Golem was sending him on a journey. But where to? Could *that which is* be the Master Golem, the god of the game? You probably had to type a letter in each box to form a kind of password.

"Five letters," he muttered. He had to screen his eyes from the glare of the star. Suddenly the image disappeared, as if the game was fed up of waiting.

He decided to check his emails. Had Albert been trying to get in touch? A blue figure in brackets showed there were twelve new messages in Hugh's in-box. And all twelve were from Albert, care of

Cyberstation, an Internet café in Moreland Town. Hugh opened the last one.

> Jeez, don't you ever check your emails?
> I have to see you. I'll be at the Cyber
> every afternoon this week. Get over
> here, or I'll turn up at your place.

Hugh smiled faintly. I expect you need more money, my friend, he thought. Let's make a deal. The money for the password.

Albert was hanging out. He ate his meals at the Moreland Arms and killed time in Cyberstation. The money Hugh had lent him had soon disappeared. But he didn't dare show up at the wimp's place again. The guys from B Corp were still in the neighbourhood and he didn't want to lead them to Hugh.

Albert was hanging out and hopping mad. When was the wimp, as he called him, going to check his emails? That afternoon he was waiting at the cyber-café as usual. He was slouched against a wall, chewing the end of a used match. Badly shaven, a crumpled suit draped over his six foot three rugby player's frame, he had become a familiar sight to the regulars. Every so often, one of the gamers would invite him to grab the controls for a round of Half-Life. The kids called him Freeman, after the game's hero. His other pastime was ogling the legs of the café's two waitresses, while dreaming of Nadia Martin, the science teacher at Moreland School.

When Hugh pushed open the door, he was greeted by a loud "Fool! Who's messing with me?" The question wasn't addressed to him. He spotted a cluster of teenagers playing Counter-Strike on the network.

"Go for it!" shouted somebody.

"Yeah, right. It keeps freezing."

Sitting with their backs to one another, the kids were calling out from their screens. There were volleys of shots from all sides.

"Don't mess with me, Devil! I nearly had him."

"Let me have a go, Mickey. Aargh, ma-aa-an! Don't shoot!"

There were peals of laughter as the gamer got pelted by bullets.

"Nasty!" Hugh chuckled. He let out a contented sigh. This was his kind of place. Gamers and computers lined up. Young guys playing at terrorists and lawmakers, their faces lit up one moment and twisted the next.

Albert was now perched on a stool by the bar. He raised an eyebrow when he saw Hugh. That was all. The young teacher sat down without looking at him.

"About time," grumbled Albert.

Hugh ordered two coffees.

"I need more money," Albert announced, staring straight ahead.

"You don't say. I'm not a millionaire, you know."

"You don't say."

"I've got to talk to you," Hugh added. But he didn't know where to start. The golem in the basements? Or the password in the star?

"Business first," said Albert. He stuck out his hand.

"I want the password for the star."

Caught off guard, Albert stared at the wimp.

"You weren't straight with me the other day," Hugh snapped. "You told me you hadn't finished the game!"

"Lower the volume," muttered Albert, glancing anxiously round. "I didn't finish the game, and that's the truth."

"So what about the star sequence? And I am that which is known by another name? What's that about?"

Albert frowned at his coffee.

"Aargh, man! Not again!" shouted one of the gamers.

The cyber corner let out a groan of despair. Counter-Strike had just been interrupted.

"It's that game that keeps hijacking the network," commented one of the waitresses.

And the cyber corner shouted, *Golemmmm!*

Albert spun round on his stool. "Let's split," he whispered.

"Attaboy, Freeman!" the gamers called on his way out.

Albert raised his hand in reply, like a Native American chieftain. Once they were out in the street, he spat out the remains of his chewed-up matchstick. Hugh couldn't help being secretly impressed by this IT wizard who looked like a tramp.

"OK," said Albert. "What are you on about this time? A star in a password, is that what you said?"

"No, the opposite." Hugh outlined the sequence and repeated the riddle.

"*I am that which is known by another name.*" Albert sniggered. "You've been smoking the wacky baccy, my friend!"

Exasperated, Hugh grabbed him by the collar. Albert didn't flinch, just gave him a pitying look. He seemed to be sulking, but in fact he was starting to take the teacher seriously. "I believe you," he admitted. "But you'd better believe me too. I didn't program that scene."

"So who did?"

They set off side by side, towards Hugh's flat.

"It sounds like a sequence that only happens on my computer," mused Albert. "Somebody must have inserted it while I was still at HQ." He'd suspected as much. Now he was sure. Somebody had been tampering with his PC behind his back.

"But who?"

"If I knew that, my little screen mate..." Albert smiled.

Hugh registered the fact he'd been called a little screen mate in silence. If Albert thought he could underestimate him, he'd got another think coming.

"Victor Dalmart!" Albert shouted suddenly.

"That's who it was?"

Albert nodded, remembering a brilliant programmer who'd worked at B Corp HQ in the office next to his. Dalmart had always asked a lot of questions. Too many. And then, one day, he'd vanished. Nobody knew if he'd come to the end of his contract or been fired. "His family lives in Festerville."

They had reached the entrance to Hugh's redbrick apartment block. Albert knew he was taking a risk, but he badly wanted a shower.

"I've got to look up Dalmart's number," he told Hugh. "Can I do it at your place?" He was trying to be more polite. The wimp needed careful handling.

But then Hugh said, "Luckily for you, my mother's out."

"You what?" Albert laughed. "You still live with your mum?" It was difficult not to make fun of Hugh. And anyway, Albert couldn't forget that Nadia Martin had fallen for him.

Hugh found a number for Dalmart, and Albert dialled it.

"Hello?"

"Mrs Dalmart?"

"It's her daughter. Who is this?"

"A ... friend of your father's," said Albert. "Is Victor there?"

Silence.

"My father's dead. Would you like to speak to my mother?"

"Er ... no, no," Albert stammered. "I'm sorry. I didn't know. He looked perfectly healthy the last time I saw him..."

"He had a car accident. On his way home from Switzerland."

"Really? Well, there you go – I mean, please accept my deepest condolences." Albert hung up, muttering, *"On his way home from Switzerland."* He looked at Hugh. "We're out of luck. He's dead."

"So I gathered. Look, Albert, there's some pretty weird stuff going on at the moment. I've got to talk to you. Down in the basements—"

Albert cut him short. "And I've got to talk to you. About B Corp."

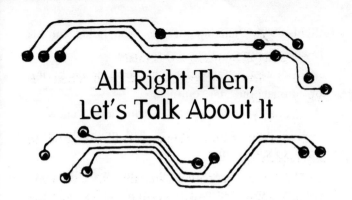

All Right Then, Let's Talk About It

The Big B Corporation. As far as Klaus the albino was concerned, until today those words stood for the people behind the scenes, the ones who gave the orders for the robberies and murders to be carried out. But now he was going to meet the head of the corporation, and he wasn't looking forward to it.

The B Corp helicopter was flying rather too low over the Swiss Alps for Klaus's liking. And, strapped in next to him in the tiny cockpit, Jason wasn't making things any easier. There was no stopping the American pilot once he started talking. After twenty minutes in the air, Klaus knew all about his previous exploits, including his hedge-hopping flights above Vietcong guerrilla strongholds, and his rescue missions to deep-sea oil rigs.

"Life as a private pilot must seem pretty boring by comparison," he commented.

"Yeah, yeah, whatever," said Jason, chewing away at his cigarette, which had gone out. "But I still do special ops."

Klaus didn't ask for details. But he couldn't get what the American had told him about Vietnam out of his mind. The way they used to load prisoners into helicopters and dropped them into the heart of the jungle from a height of five hundred metres. A very special operation indeed.

"Watch out, Mr Klaus! Hold on tight!"

Klaus was horrified to see the mountains rushing towards them. A giant peak rose up against the blue sky. A moment later, all he could see was a huge expanse of white so bright it hurt his eyes.

"Yee-ha!"

The menacing mountain top lurched to the left. Klaus felt his stomach rise up into his mouth. The blinding rays of the sun hit him like a physical blow.

Jason laughed. "The last time I did that, the door

was open. Let's hope he landed in snow, or he'd have done himself some serious damage. Ha ha!"

Klaus decided it was best not to ask *who* had landed in snow. He just pretended the joke was funny. If it *was* a joke.

The helicopter was now flying over green valleys, grazed on by cows that produced the milk for Gruyère cheese. Klaus was ruminating too. He was thinking bitterly that he only had a few minutes left to prepare his defence. He hadn't just failed, he'd been made to look a fool. His mission? To get back the electric blue New Generation BIT computer, avenge Sven's death and find his mobile phone, and last but not least track down Albert. Result? Lumps and bumps. Total humiliation.

He had no choice but to make up a story. Unfortunately, he'd never been big on imagination.

Without registering the beauty of the landscape below him, Klaus spotted a small lake fed by the Sarine River, as well as the castle belonging to the counts of Gruyères which towered over the fortified town. Jason headed towards the double peak of Broc's Tooth. There was nothing to suggest that this peaceful valley was home to the headquarters of the all-powerful Big B Corporation.

Jason landed the helicopter on the concrete roof of a bunker. Klaus jumped out and ran towards the security door, head down against the gusts whipped up by the helicopter blades. The huge building, three quarters buried beneath the rock, was right below his feet. A cross between Fort Knox and the Pentagon. The reinforced door closed behind him. Klaus hadn't been invited to use the VIP entrance. He was going in via the goods lift. It was a short, sheer drop.

A uniformed security guard was waiting for him, a holstered gun plainly visible on his hip. "Your hair's a mess, sir."

Klaus quickly smoothed his white hair back into place. He rolled his shirtsleeves down and checked the creases of his trousers. He needed to make a good impression. His appearance had to be faultless.

Because nothing else was.

The security guard gave him clearance to go through a glass door leading to the main entrance. Here I am, thought Klaus. Here I am, still alive. If they'd wanted to get rid of me, that Yank would have dropped me into a crevasse.

Inside, each green plant was a forest of hidden bugging devices. A camera lens glinted above each painting. Klaus forced a relaxed smile onto his face and made himself breathe slowly. Rumour had it that all visitors whose heart rate exceeded ninety beats a minute were killed on the spot. Smart card in hand, he made his way to the rear of the entrance hall and inserted the piece of plastic into the smart-card reader. A green indicator lit up. There was a click, and the door opened. He walked into the airlock of a double-entrance security door.

"Hello," announced an impersonal voice. "Welcome to the Big B Corporation."

There was another click and Klaus jumped. He turned round nervously. It was nothing. Just a hatch that had opened in the wall.

"Please deposit your weapons here," the voice requested.

Klaus removed the gun from under his jacket. He'd been expecting this, of course, but he was still reluctant to be separated from it. From now on he was at their mercy.

"You have not deposited all your weapons."

He groped around in his pockets and found a knife.

"Thank you. The Big B Corporation hopes you have a pleasant stay."

So do I, thought Klaus. But he wasn't banking on it.

The double-entrance security door led to surveillance post one, a square room with bars on its only window. Klaus was met by three guards. The first took his hand and stuck his thumb on an ink pad to get his print. The second frisked him. The third slipped the booty into a big envelope: a cigarette lighter, an emery board, a watch and a set of keys.

"You've got two hours to reclaim these objects," the third guard warned him. "After that they'll be destroyed."

Klaus knew what that meant. If I'm not out of here in two hours, I'll be destroyed, he thought grimly.

When the gargantuan reinforced door operated by hydraulic jacks started to move, he couldn't help feeling a twinge of admiration for Albert. How on earth had the guy managed to slip out without being picked up by the surveillance systems?

Klaus was now in the main hall. A receptionist was waiting for him behind a desk, a fake smile glued to her lips.

"Your card, please, sir." She typed something into her computer, and the printer ran off a sticker with a bar code. She stuck this on a visitor badge and held it out to him.

"I'm not a visitor," he complained.

A look of terror crossed the receptionist's face. "I'm sorry … I … it's just an unfortunate mistake. It's the glare off the screen." She glanced nervously up at the ceiling, which was bristling with cameras. The rejected badge went into the shredder.

"There you are, sir." The B Corp smile was back on her pale face. "Follow the red line. Show your employee badge to the screen at the end of the hall. Enjoy your stay at B Corp, sir."

Klaus was about to enter the heart of the corporation.

He found himself on a metal footbridge with an unrestricted view of dozens of small glass cages, where B Corp employees were busy at work. Every move they made inside these transparent prisons was monitored by a relay of teams down in the depths of the building.

The corridor on his left led to the warehouses. That was where the computers were tested one last time, before being sent all over the world. It was where the New Generation BIT electric blue model had been dispatched from. But Klaus didn't know any more than that. Albert had cunningly hidden the computer in the stock destined for B Corp's main UK warehouse. But there must have been a mix-up, because some idiot had delivered it to the young Badach kid on the Moreland Estate. Though whether it really had been a mix-up was another matter. What were they playing at, sending an expensive bit of equipment like that to Couscous City? This thought cheered Klaus up. That was what he'd say: it was a conspiracy.

The red line led him to double wooden doors. They looked like normal doors, but Klaus was under no illusions – they would be bombproof. This was the entrance to Mr William's private quarters. He felt his pulse quickening.

When the doors slid open, he found himself in a space like a dentist's waiting room. Except all the furniture was nailed to the floor. In case somebody tried attacking Mr William with a standard lamp? Klaus had been expecting a welcome from a heavily armed squadron. But the short man in glasses who came in was wearing a white jacket, not a uniform.

"I'm Dr Glockenspiel. Follow me, please," he said, sounding half jovial, half professional.

Confused, Klaus followed the doctor into a white office that smelt of disinfectant.

"Sit down."

Klaus sat in the huge reclining chair, and peered anxiously at the equipment above his head. "Are you going to…" He broke off. It had been on the tip of his tongue to say, "…torture me?"

"It won't take a second." Dr Glockenspiel pressed a button. Klaus suppressed a gasp of surprise. The chair tilted back while a helmet was lowered over his head, like one of those dryers at the hairdresser's.

"Don't move now," ordered the doctor. "There you go. Just a quick X-ray."

"An X-ray?"

"A simple precaution. Cyanide in a hollow tooth, and the like. We've seen it all before. Push your sleeve up."

Dr Glockenspiel was holding a syringe. That scary word was still echoing inside Klaus's head: *cyanide*. "What are you going to do to me?" he whimpered.

"Nothing to worry about. Just a few drops of blood."

"Ouch!" The needle had entered a vein in his arm.

"I'm going to leave you alone for a moment," the doctor announced, looking at the contents of the syringe with satisfaction.

Klaus suffered five long minutes of pure terror, convinced a deadly poison was spreading through his body. Why was his forehead on fire when his feet were frozen? Why was it so hard to breathe? Was his heart slowing down?

"Everything's in order, young chap!"

Klaus nearly jumped out of his skin. Dr Glockenspiel was back, a big smile on his face.

"You do realize," the doctor confided, "that Mr William has never had mumps. Or measles. We need to avoid all possible risk of infection."

Dr Glockenspiel showed Klaus out of his office. The red line began again. Klaus followed it. One last door. One last disembodied message.

"Approach the blue circle. Enter the blue circle.

Do not step outside it. Do not move. Do not speak unless asked to."

Klaus found himself in the middle of a room covered from floor to ceiling in brightly coloured murals celebrating B Corp's star products. Looking up, he saw a giant tub of fluorescent green farting goo glowing alarmingly like the real thing.

A strange noise like the sound of castors announced the arrival of Mr William from a long way off. Accompanied by his butler, Orwell, the head of the Big B Corporation made his grand entrance.

Klaus shuddered. The rumours were true. Mr William was so fat he went around in an over-the-top vehicle that closely resembled a baby bouncer. But it was a motorized baby bouncer, big as a Smart car, with lots more options and features. Depending on his mood, he could start up the engine or make his little legs waddle along. Legs that no longer supported his obese baby's body: Mr William was under five foot, but he weighed twenty-two stone. The boss's bald head and chubby face made him look ageless. Klaus watched him open his mouth wide and throw in a handful of pink sweets. He chewed for a moment and then spat them out.

"They're horrid!" He stamped his foot. "Yummy B strawberries taste horrid! They're not as good as the Tagada brand. I feel humiliated!"

"Mr William," whispered Orwell, "I think that Klaus…" The butler was as tall and thin as his boss was short and fat.

"Silence!" Mr William pressed a few buttons on his baby bouncer control panel with his podgy fingers. "I want Tagada!" he whined.

"You'll have sacks of them," promised Orwell.

"Sacks? I don't just want a few Tagada. I'm talking total Tagada takeover. Get it? That's the order. Let them name their price. Every kid in the world will eat Yummy B Tagada."

"That's wonderful," Orwell agreed. "But our friend Klaus must be wondering what all this is about."

Mr William looked up, apparently noticing the albino for the first time. Klaus stiffened and clicked his heels. An old German habit.

"Mr William will hear your report now," said Orwell.

Klaus cleared his throat. "The New Generation BIT computer is in a tower block on the Moreland Estate. I've located it in a flat belonging to a North African family, the Badachs."

"Cut the speeches," Orwell said softly. "We already know that."

"Er, yes, of course."

"What Mr William is wondering is why you haven't already recovered it, given that you know where it is."

"There was a counter-attack. And I suspect the traitor Albert was behind it."

"But there were two of you," Orwell pointed out treacherously, "two fully trained, armed men."

"I want him," shouted Mr William, perking up. "I want Albert!" Then he slumped back again, and stared at the screens on his console.

"I saw him," said Klaus. "He was at Big B Stores in Moreland Town. But I must warn you…"

"Yes, Klaus?"

The albino knew he had to choose his next words very carefully. "We're dealing with a conspiracy, an organized group, a network."

"Really?"

"There are eight of them, ten, I've lost count...
They're all Arabs ... all assassins... I got their
names ... and they have an enormous dog, a rabid
animal. I ... I escaped by the skin of my teeth..."

"You got their names?" asked Mr William,
suddenly taking an interest.

"Yes. Brutus. The dog, that is. Brutus. I'm sure
about that."

"Bull's-eye!" exclaimed Mr William, jabbing his
finger at one of the screens. "That's it! I've got her
now, Orwell. She's off again. Three times in two
hours. That's an infringement of regulations. Ha ha!
I've got her, Orwell."

"Yes, Mr William."

"Her file, quick, fetch me her file!" A jubilant
Mr William was punching the control panel and
making his electric baby bouncer spin round. Orwell
had produced a thick pink file which Mr William
snatched greedily. Klaus watched in amazement as
the big boss shouted, "Vaccinations all in order, no
boyfriend ... er, let's see ... allergic to angora ...
plays Internet lottery ... takes rumba classes ...
never eats celery in the canteen ... ha ha! Get that,
Orwell, no celery... Calls her mother on her mobile

during working hours… She's finished!"

Klaus had a brainwave. "The mobile!"

"Yes?" said Orwell patiently.

"Sven's mobile. I know where it is. I've got the name! Ben Azet, Samir Ben Azet. He's the guy who stole it. A kid, a scumbag from the Moreland Estate."

"Good," breathed Orwell. "We're getting somewhere at last."

Mr William was thinking hard now. "Ben Azet … Samir Ben Azet." He nodded slowly. Then came the verdict. "Kill him."

"He's just a kid," Klaus protested.

A tender expression appeared on Mr William's face. "Oh, a kid. Well, in that case, kill him … gently."

Klaus looked desperately at Orwell for support. The butler shrugged. "That handset contains top-secret information. All Sven's contacts are in there. We might as well hand over a flow diagram of our security systems to the enemy. We need that phone, Klaus."

"You'll have it, sir. Give me one more chance and I promise you'll get it back."

"Fired!" shouted Mr William.

Klaus trembled before realizing the head of B Corp wasn't talking about him.

"Orwell, fire that girl for me!"

"Very well, Mr William."

"I think I'll walk back." Mr William did a shuffle with his short legs to turn the baby bouncer round, then waddled off towards his luxury living quarters.

"And bring me Ben Azet's head!" he called.

"I'll come with you," Orwell told Klaus. But the butler stopped at the door.

"I feel a bit uncomfortable about the boy," Klaus admitted. "I don't normally bump off kids."

"Mr William can get carried away. I'll try and sort this out. We don't want any problems with the authorities, do we?"

"No."

"Bring us back the computer, the mobile and our friend Albert. Alive. We need him alive. I won't be able to cover for you much longer, Klaus. It would be best for all concerned if you succeeded this time. Do I make myself clear?"

"Yes, Mr Orwell. Thank you, Mr Orwell."

Golem

The butler broke into a benevolent smile. "I'm going to give you a back-up. A guy who trained with our militia. You'll be pleased with him. I'll leave you now. I've got to call the head of personnel."

"Ah, yes … the firing. Who is it?"

"The receptionist. You must have seen her on your way in. Mr William has noticed that she absents herself several times a day to go to the toilet. Rest assured, it's a *straightforward* dismissal…"

Klaus understood perfectly. The receptionist would live to take another rumba class.

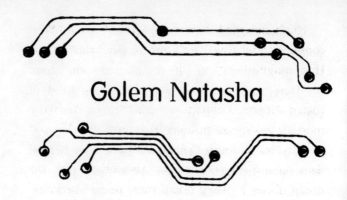

Golem Natasha

"They'll stop at nothing," Albert began. He'd have preferred to keep what he knew to himself, but he had to warn Hugh about B Corp. "Have you heard of Mr William?"

Hugh sighed exaggeratedly. "Who cares about Mr William? I'm telling you what I saw in the basements of Hummingbird—"

"You should care. You might cross paths one of these days. Nobody knows his background, but he's a psycho. I've never met him. Very few people have. Dalmart spoke to him once, and he told me about it afterwards. He was terrified. The guy's a demented pervert."

Hugh shrugged. It was the least of his worries, considering what was going on in the basements of Hummingbird—

"Don't you understand what I'm saying?" roared Albert. "Dalmart was assassinated. One life more or less means nothing to B Corp. If I'd stayed at Gruyères to finish Golem, I'd have had an accident on my way home from Switzerland too. No doubt about it. They don't want people to know what they do. At least, not *everything* they do."

Hugh was listening now. What was B Corp up to? He knew the answer. They were getting ready to launch the next generation of totally interactive computer games. Joke was a thousand times more advanced than the cyber animals currently on the market.

"I've got to tell you something you won't believe," whispered Hugh.

"There! Look!" shouted Albert, pointing at the screen.

Golem had just popped up again, launching straight into the sequence Albert claimed he hadn't designed. The starry night, the star that kept getting bigger, the rattle of the old typewriter, and the riddle:

I am that which is known by another name.

"I am that which is..." pondered Hugh. "It sounds like something from the Bible. It could be God, I suppose."

"Not enough letters. Satan would fit better: *known by another name* could mean the opposite of God." Nervously Albert typed in the five letters.

No result.

"The golem myth comes from the Jewish tradition," Hugh pointed out.

"Yeah, thanks, I knew that. Hold on... Yahweh!" Albert exclaimed. "No, too many letters. This is getting on my nerves. *That which is* means Allah, as far as your friend Majid is concerned." He typed it in. Oddly, the A and L popped up on the screen in two of the empty boxes. "Nice one!" he crowed. "*Al ... Al ... Al* what?"

Hugh reached for his dictionary to find inspiration: *album, alert, algae, alias, alibi...*

Albert sighed. "They're not necessarily the first letters."

Hugh suddenly got it. There it was, on the page

open before him. "Alias!" he shouted. "*Alias: known by another name.* That's the definition!"

"Five letters. It fits," Albert agreed.

They were both reluctant to type in the word. But the game might disappear at any time. Hugh, aka Calimero, felt numb. He couldn't tell if he was scared he hadn't found the right answer, or scared he had.

Albert solemnly spelt out each letter, striking the relevant keys.

"A-L-I-A-S... Jackpot!"

The password was now inscribed in the star. The familiar typewriter rattle followed, and the message from the beginning of the game popped up on the screen:

Enter your name.

"In the middle of a round?" Albert was surprised.

Hugh tried to intervene. But it was too late. Albert had already typed in his own name. The computer gave a pathetic ting! and switched itself off.

"Did you see that?" said Albert crossly.

"It's got a mind of its own," answered Hugh, feeling quietly smug.

Albert rebooted the computer and tinkered with the keyboard. But Golem didn't come back.

"I don't get it!" Albert was starting to lose his temper. "I can't even command my own computer, or access my own files. Everything's blocked."

"My mum'll be back soon," Hugh lied.

"There was a very clever guy at B Corp, cleverer than poor Dalmart. Granter, his name was. Used to get called out all over the world. Worked in security systems. He could help us. Problem is, he vanished into thin air. Either that or he's dead."

"Who cares?" groaned Hugh. "My mum'll be back any minute."

Albert cupped his hands. "Spare a few quid for a genius who's fallen on hard times? That's the deal, or I'm not leaving."

Hugh found his wallet and took out a note. Albert grabbed the wallet and pulled out a second one.

"Back off!" protested Hugh. "I'm not made of money!"

"Spare me the sob story. You've got a roof over your head, haven't you? And I bet Mummy pays the mortage."

Albert headed off, waving the notes in front of him.

"Moron!" muttered Hugh.

He sat down in front of his computer. He'd stay there as long as it took. All evening and all night, if need be. Sooner or later, Golem would be back.

Around ten o'clock, hunger drove him to the fridge. He switched on the coffee maker in his study and started giving himself shots of caffeine. He would hold out.

By two o'clock in the morning, his head was nodding over his book.

"A cup of coffee?" suggested his mother.

"No. No, thank you."

"It's real coffee. There aren't any lizards in it."

"What have lizards got to do with it?"

Hugh twitched violently. He'd dozed off, and a faint noise had woken him. Was it the computer or the coffee machine? The flat was silent. Just that strange smell. He gave a tired sigh and picked up his book again. A few minutes later, he glanced absent-mindedly at the screen and gasped.

Golem was there. The path, the star, the riddle.

Hugh typed in the password: **Alias**. Again the computer flashed up:

Enter your name.

Hugh knew that, for the game, he was also known by *another* name. So he entered **Calimero** in the box.

Natasha popped up instantly, but not Natasha the flirt. This was Natasha the she-warrior, brandishing her eraser-laser. She was framed by a white rectangle, and partially obscured by a fine grid pattern. Hugh frowned, wondering what kind of treatment his imprisoned girl-golem would have to suffer now.

Suddenly the loudspeakers emitted a powerful blast of air, like an air-conditioning system starting up. A beam of light, similar to the laser ray from Luke Skywalker's light-sabre, shot out from the screen. It buzzed like a giant bumblebee. *Bzzzzzz*. Hugh stood up, pushing back his chair, which collided with the pedestal table. There was a vase on it, the vase Mrs Mullins regularly filled with roses. It toppled over, spilling water on the carpet. In the confusion, Hugh shifted his gaze from the screen.

When he turned back, the beam was projecting a transparent image into the room, imprinted with a grid pattern that trembled slightly, as if a warm summer breeze was wafting through it. It was a life-size image of Natasha the she-warrior. She was standing with her back to Hugh and appeared to be floating slightly above the carpet, as unreal as a hologram. The computer made a few clicking noises. Hugh watched in alarm as the grid pattern faded and then disappeared. Click, click – the system was being fine-tuned each time. The hologram was more solid now. Light couldn't penetrate it any more. Slowly, like a swimmer struggling to reach the shore, Natasha turned round.

"Master? Master, here I am!"

The voice was distant and metallic sounding, and the words weren't synchronized with the lip movements, but they were definitely coming from Natasha's mouth. Fascinated and appalled, Hugh flattened himself against the wall. The girl-golem hadn't spotted him yet. Was she even programmed to see and identify the real world?

The beam disappeared back inside the computer with what sounded like a short intake of breath.

Natasha gave a cry of pain and liberation. She held her eraser-laser more tightly and examined her surroundings, crouching like a hunter ready to attack. Right, left…

"It's me!" yelled Hugh, realizing that she'd seen him.

Peowww! A jet of blue-white light shot out of the eraser-laser and hit him on the chest. He raised his hand to his heart. A wisp of blue smoke emerged from a hole in his shirt.

"Are you crazy? Natasha, it's me, your master!"

Peowww! Peowww! Luckily he managed to duck. Natasha looked disorientated. In the game, she blew up the enemy every time she fired her weapon.

"I'm not an Evildoer! I'm Hugh! Hugh Mullins!" He was panicking.

Casually Natasha swung her weapon over her shoulder and moved steathily forward, knees bent, hands outstretched, ready to mow down the enemy. After all, she was a black belt in karate.

"I made you!" Hugh shouted. "I'm your master. I'm Calimero!"

"Calimero?" came the robotic voice.

There was a golden flicker in her emerald-green

eyes. Was a camera linked to the computer inside that gaze?

"Calimero is our ally," intoned the girl-golem as flatly as a bad actress.

"That's right. Calimero is our ally."

If Natasha couldn't adapt to this unprogrammed situation, the safest bet was to talk to her in her own words, Hugh decided. He had read in a copy of *Joystick* that Aibo, the cyber mutt, needed hours of training before it could link the word "ball" with the object "ball". Natasha seemed to understand the sentence "Calimero is our ally", but she wouldn't be able to link the image of Hugh recorded by the camera to the name Calimero.

"Calimero is our ally," Hugh repeated.

This phrase seemed to disarm her. Could she be domesticated, like Aibo? The idea sent Hugh into spasms of excitement.

"I love you! Natasha, I love you!"

The she-warrior started advancing again. Either she couldn't identify the phrase, or she found his attitude threatening.

Hugh held up his hands in surrender. "Pretend I didn't say anything…" Then, remembering Joke, he pinned himself against the wall once more. If Natasha came into contact with him, he'd get a serious shock. But there was a puddle between him and the girl-golem. Natasha put her foot on the wet patch of carpet, and instantly there was a spray of sparks. She started crackling all over.

An explosion followed. A myriad of stars.

Then nothing.

"Natasha?"

Hugh knelt down and ran his hand over the carpet. He got a few shocks. He lay there for a moment, until a sharp pain in his chest brought him to his senses. He ripped open his shirt, sending buttons flying, and ran over to the mirror to look at his wound. It was as small as a cigarette burn, black and burning, just above his heart.

"Bad girl!" he said dreamily. He was smiling. Then he caught sight of his smile in the mirror and paused. Hands in jean pockets, shirt open exposing his wounded heart, the remains of panic in his wide blue eyes, he thought he actually looked sexy. And, for the first time in his life, he wasn't scared of looking sexy. Natasha was virtual, he knew that, but that was just another of her charms.

The rattle of the typewriter made him turn round. A message was flashing up on the screen:

Golem Natasha
size: to scale
mobility: good
vision: good
hearing: good
feeling: average
materialization: average
defence: weak
invincible armour: inoperative

The computer was compiling a report on Natasha now that she'd gone out into the world. The last line read:

number of lives remaining: 4

The Mobile Phone Changes Hands

Dr Andreas from Dial-a-Doctor was annoyed. Samir could tell from the way he was clutching his black briefcase.

"Will your mother be back soon?"

"Depends on closing time at the Moreland Arms. You might be lucky."

"Usually, when mothers ring me, they make sure they're in for my visit."

"I rang you. Don't flip, though, I've got nuff dollars. Lulu's really low. She needs something to sort her out, till I've figured out what to do about the basements. There's this thing, you get me? It's kind of hard to explain."

"Are you sure *you're* feeling OK?" The doctor looked worried.

"Fine. Apart from we've got another progress meeting coming up at school."

Dr Andreas smiled. "Right, let's take a look at the young lady, shall we?"

When they reached Lulu's bedroom door, the doctor hoicked Samir by the collar. "I don't need your help, thank you."

"She's my sister!"

But the doctor shut the door in his face. Samir put his ear to it. He couldn't make out anything for several minutes. Then Lulu seemed to come to again, and her brother heard the sound of her frail voice.

"You mustn't call him a monster. He doesn't like that."

Dr Andreas was straight into the game. "Noooo! Of course he doesn't. I wouldn't like anybody to call me a monster either. Breathe deeply, my little pumpkin."

"He kills the baddies, but he gives me the Force. I've got to go back to the basements. Your headphone thing's giving me goose pimples."

"There we go, pumpkin, all done. Can you roll over on your side for me?"

"Have you got any electric capsules for my friend?"

Dr Andreas didn't answer straight away. "Er … I always leave them in my car. They have to recharge, er … from the battery, you see."

He's got no idea about talking to little kids, thought Samir. How's Lulu supposed to know how a car battery works?

"Make sure it's not like cough medicine, OK? Because that would kill him. It's too sticky."

Dr Andreas came out and closed the door behind him. When he sat down at the living-room table, he wasn't smiling any more. "I'd rather have talked to your parents," he muttered, getting a prescription pad out of his briefcase. He scribbled a few words. "Tell them … er … that it would be sensible to consider hospitalization. I'll be honest with you, Samir. Your little sister isn't in great shape."

Samir rolled his eyes. "I can see that for myself. You don't need to be a paedophile to work that out."

There was a stunned silence.

"*Paediatrician*, if you please."

Dr Andreas put a full stop at the end of his scribbles. Samir knew his mum wouldn't bother gettting half the medicines on the list.

"By the way, I was kind of blagging it about the money. I haven't got any."

"Ah."

"But I can sort you out. I can get you a car radio, if you're interested."

The doctor laughed.

"No, seriously, they're safe radios. And you could just pay me the difference. Come off it, man, your call-out fee's less than a car radio."

The doctor snapped his briefcase shut. "I see. Now I'm the one who owes *you* money!" He walked stiffly to the door.

"Ask your mother to ring me," he said without turning round. "I've got a thing or two I'd like to say to her."

Samir sighed. Where was he going to get the money to buy Lulu's medicine? Or batteries for Joke? He scrumpled up the prescription in a fit of anger and went to look for his school bag. In it was the mobile phone he'd found by the body in the basements. An ultra-modern handset in a handsome case, the like of which had never been seen on the Moreland Estate. A mobile with a battery that never went flat.

Exactly the kind of battery Joke needed. But Samir couldn't bring himself to feed it to the monster. I'll sell it, he decided. My cousins'll go mad for it.

He looked at the gleaming piece of equipment, kissed it and put it back in his bag. It was his last hope of saving Lulu.

Nadia Martin rapped her ruler on the desk. 8D were worse than ever this afternoon. No chance of getting them interested in the mysteries of reproduction. The slightest reference to the miracle of life made the boys snigger.

"Hey, Miguel! Close your flies, we can see your pistil!"

"Wight, that's enough!" Nadia shouted. "Or we'll be discussing the wepwoduction methods of detentions!"

There was a brief lull, interrupted by the sound of a phone ringing.

"Hello? Hello?" went all the kids in a variety of voices.

"Mamadou, it's for you!" Miguel called out.

Nadia left her desk and went in search of the offending handset, which was blaring out the theme tune to Mission: Impossible. It wasn't hard to locate the source of the disturbance. Samir was on his front under his desk, both hands inside his bag.

"Sorted," he announced, straightening up. "I've stopped it."

"Give me that."

"Aargh, man. Please! I can't. It won't go off again. Promise, on my mum's head. It won't ring again."

"Hand it over. I'm confiscating it."

"But it's people messing around, you get me? It ain't fair, miss. They call me up and it's my fault."

"Mobiles are banned on school pwemises, as you well know, Thamir. Come on, hand it over."

"I can't. It's my dad's. Promise, on my dad's head…"

Nadia raised her ruler threateningly. "Hurry up!"

Samir clung to his bag. "My little sister's sick. It's so she can call me if she's feeling ill. The doctor came. He said it was serious."

Nadia tugged at the bag. Samir resisted for a moment and then let go. You wouldn't think it from looking at her, but their science teacher was hard as nails.

"It's for Lulu," he moaned. For once he wasn't lying. But Nadia had a heart of stone.

"Don't worry, I'm not going to keep it. Just ask your father to contact me. I'll hand it back to him in person."

"What kind is it?" bellowed Mamadou. "BOL?"

Nadia knew what Samir was like. And his crew too. There was every chance it *was* a BOL. In other words, it had fallen off the back of a lorry.

The flashy handset rang again and Nadia let out a cry of exasperation.

Klaus pressed the red button on his phone. The kid wasn't answering.

"You little scumbag! If it wasn't for me, *schlak*, off with your head! That's what fat boy William wanted. You owe me your life, kiddo. So answer the flipping phone!"

Klaus was even prepared to pay the brat something for the mobile. He'd decided discretion was the answer. No good showing up at the Ben Azets' and making a scene.

He started the black Volvo and headed off in the direction of the school. With any luck, he'd spot Samir coming out.

But by the time Klaus slowed down in front of the main entrance, Samir had already gone. He was pacing the concrete slabs near the Moreland Estate with Sebastian.

Sebastian pointed. "That would solve our problem."

The two boys stared at the terminal where the proud owners of an electric car were recharging its battery.

"And what's that hut place, just behind, with the flag?" Sebastian asked.

"The police station." Samir giggled. "Can you imagine the cops' faces if they saw us with Joke? 'Er, evening, Officer, just tanking up. Mad how much these electric ectoplasms guzzle, isn't it?'"

"'Just make sure you don't double-park your golem.'"

"Shut it." Suddenly Samir wasn't laughing.

"What's up with you?"

"Life sucks. I could've sold that mobile and bought medicine, and batteries for Joke. On my sister's head, if I get my hands on that crazy Martin woman—"

"The most important thing," Sebastian interrupted, "is to get Joke out of the basements. And hide him."

"Isn't there any room at yours?"

"What, like in my bed? I guess that way I could read at night."

The two boys walked slowly across Moreland Town, listing all the options they could think of. They decided against the abandoned service station, where the junkies from the estate hung out, and the town dump, which had become a supermarket for local tramps.

"The best bet," said Samir, "would be a room at Moreland Electricity."

"Got it!" exclaimed Sebastian. "The old quarry. Nobody's been back there since it collapsed." He punched Samir playfully. "Those pylons! The high-voltage line goes right through it. There's enough electricity to feed Joke for a thousand years."

"Yeah, right! And how we gonna get there?

Don't tell me – bus or taxi?"

Sebastian frowned. Joke stood out even more after dark than he did in the daytime.

"We've gotta crack this fast!" shouted Samir. "Like, really fast, because Lulu's gonna snuff it in hospital."

He wiped his eyes with his sleeve, and Sebastian pretended to tie up his shoelace, so he wouldn't see his friend crying.

"I know what I'd do if we didn't have to think about Lulu," he said, standing up again. "I'd wait till Joke was flat and run-down. Then we could just fold him up like an inflatable mattress. And – hold on! I think I'm getting an idea! Are you any good at sewing, Samir?"

Samir grabbed him by the hair and started shaking him. "Listen, blud," he spat. "You can dis me. You can call me a geek. You can even call me a fool. But nobody calls me a dressmaker. Geddit? Nobody!"

"Stop it! Saying inflatable mattress has given me an idea."

Samir calmed down.

"Camping, get it?" explained Sebastian.

"No."

"You should read Edgar Allan Poe."

"I never read," said Samir with the conviction of somebody with very strong principles.

"Well, Edgar Allan Poe's scary stuff. He wrote a story called 'The Purloined Letter'. I won't give away what happens, but the moral of the tale is: when you want to hide something, your best bet is to let everybody see it."

Joke Moves House

Aisha hesitated in the doorway, screwing up her nose suspiciously. The library was nearly empty. Miss Minx was sorting out forms, like a cashier doing her accounts at the end of the day. Towards the back, over by the window, Samir and Sebastian were pretending to flick through a pile of magazines at a small round table.

Aisha took a few steps, but she was still suspicious. "Is this a joke?" she called out.

"Shh…" The librarian made a sound like a balloon deflating. But she didn't look up.

"No, it's for real," Sebastian insisted. "Come over here."

Aisha edged a bit closer, but not too close. "Why did you want to know if I'm any good at sewing?"

Sebastian got up out of his chair and took her by the arm. "We need you."

"I'm OK with you, but I don't trust Samir. What d'you want?"

"Look."

There was a piece of paper on the table, with something sketched on it.

"We want to make a costume," Sebastian explained.

"A fancy-dress costume for the party," Samir added.

"What party?"

"Er … for the end of term…"

Aisha pulled away from Sebastian, convinced they were making fun of her. Samir and Sebastian glanced at each other in embarrassment.

"Um … it's a surprise!" Samir exclaimed. "A surprise the boys are doing for the girls. But we need your help. So you mustn't say anything, OK?"

Aisha nodded tentatively and took a look at the drawing. "What kind of costume's that?" she asked.

"A ghost," replied Sebastian.

The little Malian girl shivered. Ever since she'd seen the mysterious smoke in the corridor outside her flat, she didn't like hearing about anything weird.

"You'll have to make slippers so its feet are properly covered," Sebastian told her.

She chuckled. "I've never seen a ghost wearing slippers before."

"You ever seen one without?" quipped Samir.

"No," she admitted. "What are all those numbers for?"

"They're the measurements," Sebastian answered.

Aisha frowned. "But it's enormous!"

The two boys agreed.

"We're going to climb on top of each other. Sebastian'll go on my shoulders. So we need it as soon as, to practise."

"And what about the sheets?" she asked. "I'm warning you, you'll get in trouble. Because the sheets will be trashed."

Sebastian picked up a backpack and put it down on the table. "We had a better idea. We're making an alien ghost. A silver foil one. See?"

Aisha shrieked in amazement. This time the librarian hissed "Shh!" like a snake having its tail stepped on.

"My mum's sewing machine's gonna get brucked," Aisha continued, more quietly now. "What is that stuff?"

Sebastian unfolded a sheet of something that resembled aluminium foil. "It's a survival blanket," he told her proudly. "It's for when you're hiking in the mountains. You never catch cold."

"You can do what you like with it," said Samir. "It's non-combustible."

"You what?"

"She doesn't know what it means." Samir had only found out himself a few minutes ago. "It means fireproof."

"We've thought of everything, you see," crowed Sebastian.

"But what's the point?"

"Er..." Samir hesitated.

"You never know," said Sebastian. "A fire might break out during the party."

Aisha shrugged. Ever since she could remember, she'd helped people when they needed her. Which they did every day. So she picked up the backpack stuffed full of non-combustible survival blankets and asked no more questions.

For at least the hundredth time since becoming a hit man, Klaus cursed his parents. Why had they given birth to an albino, when it was his job not to be noticed? Everybody had turned round when he walked into the Moreland Arms to grab a bite to eat. Now he was skulking in a dark corner of the smoky bar, his face hidden behind his newspaper.

He gave himself a few minutes to reflect on his next course of action. The mobile phone, the electric blue computer, Albert ... he was pursuing lots of things. But something told him that if he could just secure one of them, the others would fall into his lap. And what about the guy he'd been promised as back-up, who hadn't showed up yet?

Lulled by the gentle hum of the conversations around him, he took a bite of his sandwich. Suddenly he pricked up his ears at the sound of a familiar name. *Ben Azet*. It had come from the bar. No question about it, the barman had clearly said, "Same again, Mr Ben Azet?" Yes, that must be him over there, the Arab guy in the green sweater. Samir's dad. "And for the missus?"

Samir's mum and dad! There they were. Could things be starting to go his way at last? With a bit of luck, the kid would be all alone in the flat at this very minute. He couldn't pass up an opportunity like that. As for proceeding cautiously: too bad. Klaus threw some money down on the table and hastily left the Moreland Arms.

His Volvo was parked a few hundred metres from the bar, not far from Hummingbird Tower. He climbed in, opened the glove compartment and took out his Magnum .357. The kid would soon remember where he'd put the mobile with that pointing up his nose.

Klaus looked up and gasped. Samir was right in front of him. He must have just come out of the main entrance to the estate. He hesitated. He couldn't risk jumping him in such a public spot. No. He'd follow him. And, seeing as it was his lucky day, maybe the kid would lead him to somebody even more interesting!

He let Samir set off before turning the key in the ignition. Nothing. He tried again. Still nothing.

Klaus swore. The Volvo wouldn't start. He kept trying angrily as he watched Samir disappear. The engine was dead. He jumped out of the car and set off at a run. Just as he was about to catch up, Samir hopped on a bus. Klaus wanted to roar with frustration.

Everybody was looking at him. Again.

"Which one are you going for?" asked Sebastian.

Samir looked at the fancy-dress outfits spread out on his friend's bed without enthusiasm. "Zorro," he decided.

"Thought so. OK, I'll be Blackbeard."

"Lulu's got an old fairy costume," said Samir. "She doesn't grow any more, because of her illness. So it should still fit her."

Sebastian had raided his parents' camping equipment. He crammed the costumes into one big rucksack and stuffed boots and gloves into another. "I'm taking a mountaineering rope too," he said. "If Joke's in a good mood, he might let us put him on a lead." He threw in a few torches and a generous supply of batteries. "For the road. In case Joke gets the munchies."

The two boys looked solemnly at each other.

"I think we're ready," said Sebastian. "Shall we go?"

Samir scowled.

Twenty minutes later, they'd made it to Samir's flat on the first floor of Hummingbird Tower.

Samir woke Lulu and gave her a handful of pills to swallow. "We're going to see Joke," he told her. "Remember what I said?"

"About moving him? I'll be sad if Joke goes."

"We're taking him to a cave full of electricity," Samir reassured her. "To get you both sparking off each other again." But he was suddenly very worried. Would the connection linking Joke and his little sister work from a distance? It wouldn't just be a few stairs separating them but more than a mile.

Samir dressed Lulu in a faded pink tulle dress and a grotty tiara. Then he put on his Zorro outfit: mask, hat and cape.

"It's a good disguise," said Lulu admiringly. "I can't tell it's you any more."

Blackbeard was waiting for them in the living room, surrounded by bags.

"I'll have to carry Lulu," said Samir. "Here, take that." He kicked a large object wrapped in plastic. Sebastian tried lifting it.

"Ouch! It's nuff heavy! What's in it?"

"A surprise. Don't forget Joke's costume."

Luckily the lift was working. They loaded everything inside and pressed the button for the ground floor.

"Keep a lookout," ordered Samir. "I'll sort the padlock."

It was that time of day when the caretaker went to Big B Stores to fill his shopping basket with discounted red wine. The main entrance hall was quiet. A bunch of keys and picks jangled in Samir's hand: a present from his cousins, on a day when they'd been in a good mood. According to them, you could open ninety per cent of locks with them. Samir put his ear to the padlock, then set to work. It only took him two or three minutes to find the right key.

"Got it! Hurry up!"

Sebastian opened the heavy wooden door and switched on his torch. The last bulb in the underground corridors had died a long time ago. Both boys were wearing wellington boots and rubber gloves to protect themselves against shocks. Lulu had been waiting patiently, slumped against a big backpack, in ballet shoes and her fairy dress. Samir scooped her gently off the ground. Sebastian went ahead, his arms full, a torch between his teeth.

Lying motionless at the back of lot 401, Joke had never been so floppy: he looked like a cross between a wrinkled old balloon and stringy candyfloss.

Samir put his little sister down and started unwrapping the large object he'd made Sebastian carry. "Look, Joke, din-dins."

"It looks like a car battery," said Sebastian.

"Funny that, bro, I was just thinking the same thing."

"Where d'you get it from?"

"Jacked it from some posh type. That'll teach him to park his flash Volvo in front of Humming-bird Tower."

Samir picked up the battery with his gloved hands and cautiously made his way over to the monster. Joke might be at a low ebb, but he still scared the living daylights out of Samir. "Easy,

Joke," he muttered. He put the feast on the floor a few metres from the monster and quickly stepped back. "Gru-u-ub time!" he called out. "Here, boy, come on…"

"We haven't got any strength left," whispered Lulu, as if she and Joke were one and the same.

The monster spread his misty shape, like a genie emerging from Aladdin's lamp.

"It's hard," sighed Lulu.

As Joke made contact with the battery, Samir lay on the ground and clutched his little sister tight. The darkness in the basements was swept away by a blast of light, like an ultra-powerful camera flash.

"Yummy! Me still got munchies!" said Joke.

"Lulu!" Samir called out for help as the palpitating creature suddenly loomed over him. The battery was giving off stinky smoke.

"Be nice!" Lulu reminded him, standing up. She wobbled and then ran towards her friend.

Sebastian was already unfolding the ghost outfit made by Aisha. "Tell him we're taking him for a walk," he ordered Lulu. "And nice monsters don't go out without any clothes on."

"Give me your paw," Lulu commanded.

"I love you," replied Joke.

"There you go," Lulu said. "He's understood."

Aisha had done a good job in so little time. Instead of being a one-piece, the outfit consisted of a ghost-wrap and an elegant pair of silver bootees. While Lulu was whispering to her darling monster, Samir and Sebastian struggled to get the bootees on his huge luminous feet.

"His feet must be at least a size twenty," said Sebastian. He was joking, but his rubber gloves were trembling. "I think his big toe might be touching the end." Remembering an occasion when a sales assistant had fobbed him off with trainers a size too small, he added, "The material's soft. It'll stretch."

Joke proved remarkably cooperative, but the boys still felt like they were dressing a giant public monument, all lit up.

"Lulu," said Samir, "can you tell him to bend down?"

"All you have to say is 'Bend down, Joke.'"

"It's pa-aa-arty time!" said Joke, whose conversation was limited by the Furby he'd swallowed.

Gently he bent down, tucked himself in and huddled up.

"When I give the signal," ordered Sebastian, "go for it!"

The giant silvery wrap engulfed Joke's podgy shape.

"Now we should be able to touch him without a thousand volts zapping through our bodies," said Sebastian, holding onto the fireproof sheet. "There you go, big boy, your eyes are opposite the holes."

Lulu tied laces around Joke's slipper boots. Samir wound the mountaineering rope round his chunky waist.

And that was how Zorro, Blackbeard, Princess Lulu and the silver foil ghost made their exit from the basements of Hummingbird Tower.

"It's stupid, your story about the stolen letter," declared Samir crossly. "The more people can see you, the more they look at you."

The team wasn't passing unnoticed through the streets of Moreland Town.

"That's the least of our worries," said Sebastian.

"Have you seen the sky?"

There were big black clouds gathering overhead. If Joke's disguise wasn't completely watertight, if a single drop of rain touched him – disaster.

"Da-aa-mn!" swore Samir. But he wasn't looking at the sky. He was watching a smiley Mrs Badach heading their way, her arms weighed down with Big B Stores plastic bags.

"Iz you, Samir? I recognize you, innit!" Emmay beamed. "And Lulu!" she exclaimed. "She iz walking!"

"Yippee-yay! It's pa-aa-arty time!"

Mrs Badach glanced up at the strange figure that had spoken, and gave it a puzzled look. "Iz most beyootiful coztume," she decided.

"Sorry, Mrs Badach," Samir said in a rush. "It looks like it's going to rain. We've got to get a move on."

"Have fun, childrin!" Dreamily Emmay watched the little group disappear. What kind of costume was that? An astronaut, maybe?

The children were relieved to leave the busy streets of Moreland Town behind. They headed out, past the car park of Roger's Garage, where a man with white hair glanced casually their way.

Klaus wasn't in the mood for a fancy-dress party. His Volvo would be out of action for at least forty-eight hours: the time it would take to order a new battery. Fortunately the back-up he'd been promised by B Corp was arriving tomorrow. The more the merrier, considering recent events. The first drop of rain plopped on his head. Klaus moved under cover and swore.

A second drop followed. But the downpour was still holding back. The children noticed Joke was showing signs of nervousness. The storm that was brewing could prove deadly.

"Let's cut through the dump." Sebastian wanted to pick up the pace, but they were hampered by Joke waddling clumsily along on the end of his leash. The ground was starting to soften underfoot, soaked by rain that was falling steadily now. At the first crash of thunder, Joke swerved suddenly and wobbled about under his silver sheet. Lulu clung on and tried to calm him down.

"The storm's too strong for you. You mustn't eat the lightning, or you'll get tummy ache."

Seeing his little sister shivering, Samir took off his Zorro cloak and draped it over her shoulders.

"We've got to find shelter!" Sebastian called out, scanning the mountains of rubbish. "He'll disconnect for good in this kind of weather."

Samir pointed to the shell of a van. "Quick!" He pulled open the battered rear door.

"Hey! What's going on?" a voice complained. "Nobody teach you to knock before entering?" A old man clutching a bottle to his chest stared at Samir with small angry eyes. "Crikey, it's carnival time! And – well I never, excuse me…" The tramp had just noticed Joke. "Welcome to my humble abode, Michelin Man. Come in, Princess, come in."

The children hauled Joke into the ramshackle vehicle. Their host looked curiously at the monster's enormous round feet, wrapped up like giant Easter eggs.

"Fancy a drop?" offered the tramp, holding out his bottle to Joke.

Joke's reaction was violent. He kicked out with a foot and an unprotected part of his body came into contact with the tramp. The poor man went flying backwards.

"Are you OK?" asked Sebastian anxiously.

The tramp opened his eyes. Terrified, he crawled to the door and tumbled out into the mud. Then he stood up shakily, glanced behind him and staggered off, snorting, "The storm's inside!"

It rained heavily for half an hour. When a patch of blue sky reappeared among the grey clouds, Sebastian suggested covering the last few hundred metres separating them from the quarry.

"We haven't got time for it to dry completely," he said. "We'll just have to watch out for puddles."

They made their way slowly, circling the edges of the waterlogged patches, treading carefully on the muddy ground. They passed the houses being demolished on the edge of the motorway. They were nearly in the countryside. The wires of the high-voltage line above their heads showed them where to go.

Red and white tape stretched between posts barred them from entering the quarry. As did a large placard.

KEEP OUT!
DANGER OF LANDSLIDE

"There isn't a real risk," Sebastian insisted. "I've heard they want to use it for outdoor shows or something."

"That's the last thing we need," grumbled Samir.

They led Joke into a huge cavern the colour of chalk.

"You'll be nice and snug in here, big boy," said Sebastian.

"Cock-a-doodle-doo! The sun's come out to play," answered Joke.

"He's fed up with his outfit," Lulu translated.

The boys quickly undressed the monster.

"We'll leave your slippers on," Sebastian told him. "The ground's still damp."

Samir stood at the entrance to the cave. He was examining the pylons. "I'll ask my cousins," he shouted back down the tunnel. "Maybe they'll know how to get the electricity to— Na-aa-ng!"

Joke had crept up behind Samir. He was also showing an interest in the long wires dissecting the sky. In fact, he was looking at them very greedily indeed.

"Joke, no!" yelled Sebastian.

Joke set off towards the nearest pylon. He climbed up it like a monkey. In a matter of seconds he was perched right on the top.

Instinctively the three children raised their arms to protect their eyes. The sun had never lit up Moreland Town and its surroundings with such a dazzling light.

"Don't eat it all!" Lulu called. "Or you'll go pop!"

The Good Old Ways

Tiny Mrs Cure was sipping her coffee and waving her minuscule hands. "I've stood up for Samir in the past," she told Nadia, "but you're absolutely right. He's gone too far this time."

"I nearly hit him on the head with my wuler," Nadia admitted. She pushed away her plastic cup and stood up.

"They may have a mobile phone, but there's no guarantee of food on the table," the maths teacher pointed out.

"I'm not worried on that score, Mrs Cure. Thamir always finds a way."

Nadia walked across the staffroom to pick up

some work from her locker. There, on top of the pile, was a white envelope. She opened it and found a note:

I owe you an apology for the other day. Would you let me make it up to you over a pizza?

Albert (the man you wanted to dissolve in acid)

He'd written his mobile number at the bottom.

"A pizza! What a jerk!"

"Is there a problem, Nadia?"

"No, it's nothing, Mrs Cure."

Nadia stuffed the note into her pocket, wondering why she didn't just rip it up. Then she picked up her work and went home.

The back-up promised by B Corp had arrived a few hours ago, and Klaus was already wishing it hadn't. He'd been expecting somebody with experience who could support him in the firing line. He'd been sent a greasy, long-haired guy who was fat and dirty. Klaus had taken an instant dislike to Eddie the overgrown teenager, with his check shirt buttoned up the wrong way and his shoelaces undone. He said he was a technician.

Eddie and Klaus were now sitting in the back of a vehicle that resembled a TV production van, with all its screens and knobs and levers, not to mention the satellite dish on the roof. Great if you wanted the kids on the estate to swarm around you like flies.

Eddie was giving Klaus a quick lesson, talking to him like he was a child. "Right, I'm going to demonstrate how we track a mobile. As you'll see, in five minutes we'll know exactly where it is."

"Samir Ben Azet," Klaus grunted. "Thirteen years old. Class 8D, Moreland School. Alcoholic parents. Lives in Hummingbird Tower, first floor. Remember, I got here before you, kiddo."

"Congratulations, Mr Klaus," replied the young technician in a voice as infuriating as it was respectful. "OK, Samir Ben Azet. It'll only take me a few minutes and I'll be able to tell you which pocket he carries his phone in."

Klaus shook his head disbelievingly.

"I'll also be able to tell you everywhere he's been in the last two days," Eddie threw in for good measure.

An aerial map of Moreland Town appeared on

a screen. A small cross was flashing. Eddie probably fancied himself as a pilot about to zap Hummingbird Tower, thought Klaus sourly.

"Mobiles give off a signal," Eddie explained. "The phone points pick up the signal and send it to the phone company, which keeps a record of the data for a year."

"And what d'you do?" asked Klaus. He was secretly getting interested.

Eddie laughed as he tapped away at his console. "Me? I've got access to the works. I can tell you where our friend is right now, I can tell you where he was yesterday at 4.30 p.m., I can tell you if he made or received any calls. You want it, I can do it."

The young technician typed in the number of the mobile phone stolen from the unlucky Sven. The picture zoomed in on an area of Moreland Town. Klaus was surprised to see the tall tower blocks of the estate thinning out as the map headed northwards, towards the train station.

"Wrong direction," Klaus pointed out smugly. "Hummingbird Tower's not in that neighbourhood."

"Maybe the kid doesn't always stay on his own patch."

An area of residential streets with smart suburban houses and low-rise apartment blocks appeared on the screen. It didn't make sense. What would a Ben Azet be doing there? Eddie was just a technician. He didn't ask questions like that. He trusted the information he got. End of story.

"Voltaire Street," said the technician.

The picture focused in more sharply.

"There we are. Got it. Number 28."

"So?" grouched Klaus. "Where's this getting us?"

A list of names appeared on the screen.

"All the residents at number 28," said Eddie. "There are eight flats. Shall I dial the number?"

"No point," Klaus replied. "The kid never answers."

But Eddie wasn't so easily discouraged. After three rings, somebody did answer.

"Hello?"

It was a woman's voice. Eddie signalled to Klaus to speak into the microphone in front of him. Klaus was caught off guard.

"I … er…" he stammered. "Sorry, must have got the wrong number."

"Mr Ben Azet?" came the voice.

"Ben Azet," Klaus repeated, increasingly confused. He didn't need to say any more. The person on the other end had plenty to say.

"I'm weally sorry, Mr Ben Azet, but mobiles are banned on school pwemises. I wanted to teach Thamir a lesson, but I don't want you to think... Look, I've got a class with 8D tomorrow morning. I'll happily give your phone back to Thamir then. If you could just make sure he doesn't bring it to school any more. I hope you're not angwy with me, but those are the wules... Mr Ben Azet?"

"Er, yes..." For a moment, everything went fuzzy in the van. "No, wait!" Klaus shouted. "I don't even know your name."

"Miss Martin. Thamir's science teacher," said Nadia, sounding surprised. "Didn't he tell you?"

"Yes, of course. Listen, Miss Martin, I need my phone back urgently, but I don't want you to go to any trouble. Could we meet outside your apartment block in ten minutes, say?"

"Er ... but ... yes, I mean ... yes. All wight."

Klaus hung up and shot young Eddie a triumphant look. "See, kiddo," he said patronizingly, "you've got all the flash gear, but where does it get you? In ten minutes, this lady'll be handing over the mobile, easy as pie. If we'd done it your way, we'd still be fiddling with one of your satellite gizmos, wouldn't we? The good old ways, Eddie, they're still the best. Come on, start the engine."

Eddie was looking at him oddly. "Excuse me, Mr Klaus…"

"What?"

"She didn't give you her address."

"But we've got it! Voltaire Street. You're the one who found it. See, I remember this stuff."

"Yes, I know we've got it. But she didn't give it to you."

Klaus's complexion was so white, he couldn't turn any paler. "I'll tell her I looked her up in the phone book. Listen, you're starting to get on my nerves. Step on it, will you?"

Eddie drove off very slowly, as if worried he might lose his train of thought. "She might suspect something. Especially since you didn't know her name."

"Put your foot on the accelerator!"

Eddie gave the engine more juice. But not much. "It's an Arabic name, Ben Azet," he remarked. "She must have noticed you didn't have much of an accent."

"So? Plenty of Arabs speak excellent English. I'm warning you, we don't tolerate racists at B Corp."

Eddie nodded. But he was not to be diverted. "What about when she sees you? Would it be racist to point out you don't really look like an Arab?"

Klaus gave the kid a nasty smile. "Don't you know *anything*? Arab albinos are the same colour as Swedish albinos and Brazilian albinos. White. Just drive!"

This time Eddie really did put his foot on the accelerator. He even allowed a good minute or so to go by before adding, "Teachers generally get to meet the parents of their students. I wonder if she'll recognize you?"

Nadia burst out laughing. She was standing all alone on the pavement in front of 28 Voltaire Street.

How silly of me! I forgot to give him my address, she thought. What should she do now? Poor old Mr Ben Azet could zigzag across town for days before tracking her down. He was probably too embarrassed to call back. Samir's dad had come across rather well on the phone. Strange, since there was never a good word said about the Ben Azet family in the staffroom.

She examined the mobile awkwardly. A model like that must have cost a small fortune. Suddenly she had a flash of inspiration and started pressing some buttons experimentally. After a few unsuccessful attempts she hit the right key, the one that brought up the address book. People often stored their home number. Nadia pressed twice on the *abc* key, to reach the Bs, and scrolled down the list of names.

Nothing. No Ben. But there were other names. Lots of them. All nationalities. Weird. Some of them looked like German names, others French. Nadia wasn't sure why, but she felt ill at ease. Mr Ben Azet seemed to know a lot of people. Vaguely ashamed about being so nosy, she kept scrolling through the phone book. There were Chinese, Japanese and even Indian names...

"Duh!" she exclaimed. "Azet! I need to look under A."

She pressed the *abc* key once, to call up the list

of names starting with A. The first name to appear on the small screen was familiar. *Albert*.

"How funny," she murmured.

But so what? The Ben Azets probably had a friend called Albert. Nadia studied the number and frowned. She still had the note in her pocket. She fished it out. Glancing at it, she shuddered. It was the same. What connection could there possibly be between the wretched Albert and Samir's family?

Curiosity's getting the better of me, she thought. I'm suddenly in the mood for a pizza. Then, if Albert really does know Mr Ben Azet, he can give me his home number. Yes, that's it, that's why I'm calling him, Nadia told herself as she pressed the green key.

A deep voice answered. "Hello?"

"Sorry to disturb you," Nadia began, "but—"

"Who's calling? Who is this?"

Nadia was taken aback. The tone was brutal, almost hateful. "Nadia Martin. The woman who—"

"Where are you calling from? Whose mobile have you got there?"

"I must have made a mistake. I—"

"Nadia? Is it really you?"

"Yes," she sighed.

No answer. Silence.

Distracted, Nadia watched a van pull up on the opposite side of the street.

"You're using a BIT handset," said the voice. "Where the hell did you get that piece of junk?"

"I don't understand. Are you … Albert?"

"Where did you get that phone?"

"It's not mine. I confiscated it from a student, and now I'm waiting to give it back to his dad. I've awanged to meet him."

"You're out of your mind! Where are you?"

"In the street, of course. I think that's him I can see now. Or them. There are two of them. They're looking my way."

"Who? D'you know them? What do they look like?"

"There's a funny-looking guy, a bit like an … albino, and the other—"

"Run!" Albert yelled.

"What?"

"Run, Nadia. Fast!"

This was crazy. Ridiculous. She wanted to burst out laughing. But when she saw the albino stretching out his arm towards her, she started running.

A quick glance over her shoulder confirmed that the two men were chasing her. But when she was younger — not that much younger, in fact — Nadia had come fourth in the regional final of the one hundred metres. She clutched the mobile like a relay baton. Without slowing down, she held it to her ear.

"Nadia, where are you? What's going on?"

"Voltaire Street. I can't see them any more," she panted. "I think … I think … they've gone back to their van."

"Don't stop. Run! Where are you now?"

Nadia grunted as she bumped into a man walking his dog. "I'm … I'm turning into Nelson Mandela Square."

"I'm coming to meet you!" shouted Albert. "Make for the station. Can you see them?"

"No!"

Nadia nearly got run over by a moped as she crossed the square. She was starting to feel a sharp jabbing pain in her groin. Why didn't I just go back indoors? she wondered. She tripped and clutched the arm of a fat lady with a purple rinse to stop herself falling. Everybody was staring. Her worst nightmare.

"Can you see them?"

"No! Yes! They're coming!"

"Take the next side street, to the right."

"Where? Oh yes, I see." She veered off sharply. The driver of the van was caught out. "I can't go on…" Nadia slowed to a walk for a few metres before sprinting off again, galvanized by Albert's voice.

"Run! Run, Nadia. I'm coming to find you. Where are you?"

"The … the avenue."

"Sycamore Avenue?"

"Yes…"

"Cross the road. Head for the footbridge. Can you see them?"

Nadia glanced fearfully behind her. She spotted the satellite dish rising up out of the traffic. The van was stuck.

"They're jammed… They're … they're going up onto the pavement."

"Forget about the bridge. Go to the roundabout, Nadia. Quickly!"

She started running again. Ten metres, twenty metres. She pulled up abruptly, doubled over. She straightened up, turned round. The two men had abandoned their vehicle and were coming towards her, pushing people roughly out of the way.

"Albert ... Albert!"

There they were. Nadia saw the albino slip his hand into his pocket. Something told her there was a weapon in it.

"Albert!" she breathed.

"Nadia!"

She didn't realize at first that his voice was no longer coming from the mobile.

"Get in! Hurry up!"

A car door swung open in the middle of the road, prompting a chorus of shouts and blaring horns. Nadia swerved, narrowly escaping the grasp of a fat kid with long greasy hair. She dived inside the car.

Albert drove off, in a hail of expetives.

He dodged silently in and out of the traffic, his eye on the rear-view mirror. Next to him Nadia was trying to get her breath back. She couldn't understand how she'd managed to wind up next to a complete stranger, being chased by two hit men.

Albert didn't relax until he'd left the tower blocks and streets of Moreland Town far behind.

"I think you owe me an explanation!" said Nadia.

"I'm not sure I know what's going on," confessed Albert. "Basically, what matters is— Oh no, they're back!"

Nadia let out a squeal of terror. Albert had just accelerated like a maniac, pinning her back in her seat. A hundred metres further on, he turned sharply into a potholed road. The little car bounced from bump to bump, sending clods of mud flying into the ditch.

"They've put the techies on to it! The mobile, Nadia!"

"The techies? What d'you ... they're following us ... they're going to—"

"The mobile!" he roared.

Nadia handed it over. Albert slowed down briefly and chucked the handset into a puddle. Seconds later he dug out his own mobile and repeated the procedure.

"What are you doing? Are you cwazy?"

"Don't you understand?" he yelled. "They're tracking us. We might as well have flashing lights strapped to the car."

"Watch out!" screamed Nadia.

A fence barred the road in front of them. Albert charged it, trailing posts and barbed wire behind them. To their left a winding road led towards a wood.

A couple of miles on, he finally took his foot off the accelerator. "They'll have realized by now that I've got rid of the mobiles," he announced. "They must have given up."

"Are you sure?" She took a deep breath. "Albert?"

"Yeah?"

"What's happening? I don't understand any of this."

"I'm the one who should be asking the questions. How did you get hold of that mobile?" Albert accelerated in his agitation.

"Please, don't get angry."

He slowed down again as they reached a crossroads, chose a path heading into the wood, and drove on until they reached a sunny clearing.

"Nadia," he said softly, "that was a BIT handset. From the Big B Corporation."

"From the Big B Corporation," she echoed.

"There's a sign that pops up on the screen when the call's from a phone issued by B Corp, d'you understand?"

"No. And I think my heart's going to explode. I can't get my bweath back. Did they really want to kill me?"

"Of course they didn't. They wanted to kill *me*."

"You? Who *are* you? A criminal?" She shuddered. He put his arm round her. "Are you going to explain all this?" she asked.

She looked up. Albert's face was very close.

At that very moment, the van came to the crossroads and went down a tarmac road between the trees.

"Still nothing?" asked Klaus from the driver's seat.

Eddie's voice came from behind. "We've lost them. The mobiles aren't transmitting a signal any more."

"That's technology for you!" sniped Klaus.

He slowed down and parked on the verge, in the shadow of the trees. "I thought it was supposed to be idiot-proof," he complained, climbing out of the van.

"They must have destroyed the handsets. I'm not receiving anything."

"I'm going to take a leak," said Klaus, pushing his way into the thicket.

A minute later Eddie joined him in the bushes, bracken and brambles.

"A satellite dish on the roof," Klaus cursed, buttoning his flies. "Why not have a siren while you're at it? If we'd done this my way, I'd have turned up nice and discreet, and little Miss Martin would've handed over her mobile just like that. The good old ways, my friend, the good old ways."

"They've failed, Mr Klaus," said Eddie politely. "As far as we're concerned, they've had their day."

"They've what?"

Klaus turned round. Young Eddie was pointing a gun at him.

"*As far as we're concerned?*" Klaus repeated in a wobbly voice. "What d'you mean, *we*?"

"Game's over, Mr Klaus. The whole town's seen

you now. Sorry, but I'm under orders. I really am very sorry."

Eddie fired twice. It's the kind of death Mr Klaus would have wanted, he thought. *Bang! Bang!* The good old way.

Nadia pushed Albert away. "What was that? Did you hear something?"

"Hunters," he replied.

"I hate hunters."

"Me too," Albert agreed. He put his arm round her again, as if trying to reassure her. Then he whispered in her ear, "You wouldn't have some change on you, sweetheart?"

"Change? Yes. Why?"

"I've got to go to a car wash. I haven't got my own vehicle at the moment, you see. I had to, er, borrow this one, and it's all muddy. I wouldn't like to hand it back in this state."

"A con artist," sighed Nadia. "That's what you are."

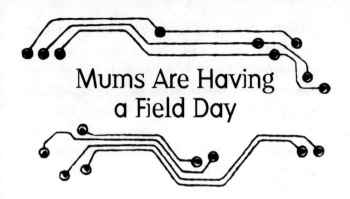

Mums Are Having a Field Day

Back in her kitchen, Mrs Badach was still laughing about those children in their fancy-dress outfits. Emmay had sometimes seemed strict and talked crossly when she was bringing up her seven boys, but deep down she loved parties, practical jokes and tender moments. The mint tea was steaming in her glass when the doorbell rang. She wiped her hands swiftly on her apron. Somebody was dropping by for tea! She put a plate of biscuits on the kitchen table and hurried to open the door.

"*Macha Allah!*" Mrs Badach was so overcome with emotion she had to grip the door frame to stop herself toppling over. "Haziz!"

In front of her stood the son who'd run into trouble on the estate, the son the police had arrested for dealing in jacked mopeds. The son she loved so much, but who'd never been seen since. Emmay stroked his jacket. It was premium leather.

"Is Dad around?" Haziz asked fearfully. He was a strapping man now, but he still remembered his dad's beatings.

Emmay shook her head and smoothed the sleeve of his designer jacket with her hand. "You iz looking smart," she said softly, while her heart was shouting, *Haziz, my son, my light!*

"Yeah, things are going OK," the young man muttered as he walked in. He glanced edgily around the living room. Hands in pockets, shoulders hunched, he still looked shifty, as if he might have to make a quick getaway. He caught a whiff of the familiar smell of mint tea and a smile briefly lit up his bony, bumpy face.

"I've got a job now," he announced, standing tall again.

"Iz good, my son."

He was pirating software, recording CDs and masterminding a trafficking operation in nearby

Rokaz. "In computers," he added.

"Iz good," Emmay said again.

They went into the kitchen. Haziz saw the gazelle horns on the plate and a wave of nostalgia washed over him.

"Emmay..." Haziz was struggling for words. Always being on the wrong side of the law, raves, babes, stealing, cheating, lying low. It wasn't a life. Not a life a man could tell his mum about. "Please forgive me," he said, so quietly you needed a mother's ears to hear him.

"Iz Allah who forgive," said Emmay. And then the most beautiful smile ever seen on the Moreland Estate spread across her face. "I love you, my son. To sit." And without saying a word about all those days of waiting, all those nights of crying herself to sleep, Emmay poured him some mint tea.

"Where's Majid?" Haziz asked. He hadn't forgotten his little brother. The shortest and cheekiest of the Badach boys.

"Iz back soon," said Emmay. "He will be so happy."

"Yeah, but I can't wait around much longer." Haziz didn't want to see his dad.

Luckily Majid was on time, and overjoyed to see him. The two brothers went "Touch, blud!" and there was a lot of "You all right? W'happen?" Haziz proudly informed his younger brother that he was organizing a massive games tournament, sponsored by Big B Stores. A whole weekend of people slaughtering each other at Counter-Strike.

This weekend.

"Cyberstation's lending us thirty PCs," Haziz explained. "And players can bring their own. We're going to hook everybody up to the network. There'll be a giant screen you can follow the games on, a bar, merguez sausages. You can even sleep over. The works."

Majid's eyes were popping out of his head. "Wicked! My English teacher's gonna be well into that," he added.

Haziz looked at him suspiciously. Since when had Majid become a geek? "You'd be better off telling Samir's cousins about it."

Emmay frowned. Miloud and Rachid had a very bad reputation on the estate. But Haziz explained you were better off having guys like that on your side. "Otherwise they'll kick up trouble."

"Where you iz having your mega party?" asked Mrs Badach.

"We've found a heavy spot," said Haziz. "The quarry!"

While Mrs Badach was being reunited with her long-lost son, Mrs Mullins was getting ready to see her son again too. She'd made a snap decision at her sister's. Her flat was haunted and she was going to move. She wanted to let Hugh know her plans as soon as possible.

Hugh, on the other hand, was getting ready for a second encounter with Natasha. Armed with a water pistol, he sat down at his keyboard and typed in **Alias** followed by **Calimero**. Then he leant back in his chair. Just as before, the hologram was projected into the study. But when the grid pattern disappeared, Natasha looked more solid and opaque. More real. Her clothes – a low-cut strappy top and skimpy shorts – hugged her figure like a second skin. Ten small flasks hung from her belt. The eraser-laser looked like a natural extension of her arm.

As soon as the shaft of light set her free, Natasha

turned round slowly. She saw Hugh. "Calimero is our ally," she intoned.

The young teacher nodded gently, keeping his hands in his pockets.

"I have come to destroy B Corp," added the she-warrior.

Hugh wondered if he'd heard right. Why, in a game produced by B Corp, would a character talk about destroying B Corp? "Is that your mission?" he asked, unsure to what extent the computer could interpret and understand his words.

"My mission," chanted Natasha, "is to destroy B Corp."

Peowwww! Peowww! Two blue-white rays shot out of the eraser-laser, one of them hitting a confiscated Puff Z Sniddy CD, the other an empty can of Big B cola.

"Let's just cool it," said Hugh, his right hand gripping the water pistol.

"Master, master!" Natasha called out. "B Corp has invincible armour. I need a mega-powerful weapon."

Peowwww! She fired again, making a hole in a book.

"I'm the master around here!" shouted Hugh.

"So stop wrecking my things!"

Instantly he regretted his mood swing. Natasha was aggressive. He couldn't afford to forget that. The girl-golem was heading towards him, an alarming glint in her green eyes.

"Wait, I'm your ally. Calimero is your ally!" he gabbled desperately.

"Calimero is our ally," said Natasha, coming to a halt centimetres away from him. In the game she'd got a top-of-the-range IQ but in real life she didn't seem very bright.

"Why d'you want to destroy B Corp?" Hugh asked her.

"That is my mission."

They were going round in circles.

"Is Alias your master?"

"The Master Golem is called Alias. Calimero is our ally. My mission is to destroy B Corp."

"I guess that's a clear enough summary," muttered Hugh. But then he heard a noise that made the blood drain from his face.

It was the sound of the front door opening.

"Hugh!" called Mrs Mullins. "It's me. I'm back... Hugh?"

"Be with you in a minute." Hugh was paralysed. He couldn't introduce Natasha to his mother. She'd flip. But he couldn't destroy her either. He remembered the computer's sinister warning: **number of lives remaining: 4**. What happened when all her lives were gone?

Hugh went up to the girl-golem and nearly put a hand on her arm. At the last moment, he drew back. "Listen to me, Natasha. I've got to go on a mission. Don't move from here." Would she understand that?

"Are you changing levels?" she asked.

"That's right, I'm changing levels," Hugh said very clearly. "I'm going to find you a more powerful weapon, and after that we'll be able to destroy B Corp."

"That is my mission," said Natasha approvingly.

Unbelievable, having a conversation with a computer character!

"Hugh?" called Mrs Mullins again.

The young teacher backed away from Natasha, whispering one last time, "Don't move." Then he turned round and slipped through his study door, shutting it firmly behind him.

"Don't tell me you were busy playing!" tutted his mother, shaking her head fondly.

"Er, yeah, right, playing," stammered Hugh.

"If you could see the state you get into." Mrs Mullins sighed. She wasn't feeling great herself, now that she was back in the flat. She went over to the sitting-room window and opened the curtains. She turned round to face her son. "A bit of ligh—"

She broke off, mouth wide open, staring at something behind Hugh.

Her son guessed what had happened, but he hadn't heard the study door open. Of course! In the game he'd granted Natasha the special power of walking through walls. He turned his head and saw the girl-golem in her shorts and strappy top, legs planted wide apart, hands on hips. It'd be difficult to pass her off as a teacher, even a PE teacher, he thought helplessly.

"Ah, yes!" he said in a strained voice. "I forgot to tell you that I invited a friend round. She's called Naaa…" His voice shook. He was losing his nerve. He coughed and tried again. "Natasha Duran."

Mrs Mullins got over her initial shock. She took

a deep breath and made an effort to be polite. "Pleased to meet you, Miss Duran…" She walked over to Natasha, her hand held out.

"No!" yelled Hugh. "She's elec— infectious."

"Infectious?" echoed Mrs Mullins. Taken aback, she examined the young woman's ample curves. Natasha looked a picture of health. But there *was* something odd about her, something missing. And what was she hiding behind her back?

"She's infectious," Hugh repeated. He opened his study door and said, "Come on, Natasha."

The girl-golem looked at him but didn't move. The order meant nothing to her.

"Come-with-Calimero," Hugh spelt out, giving his mother an irritated look.

"Calimero is our ally," said Natasha as she obeyed the order.

They disappeared back into the study, leaving Mrs Mullins standing flabbergasted in the sitting room. What on earth was this … she hesitated between "girl" and "thing". And shivered. When that … creature … had turned its back, she'd seen, quite clearly, a monstrous weapon.

On the other side of the door, Hugh grabbed hold of his swivel chair as his legs gave way.

"How many levels does B Corp have?" asked Natasha all of a sudden. There was a hint of surprise in her bad actress voice now. She was like a sleeper waking from a dream.

"We're not at B Corp. We're in my flat," Hugh said wearily, not expecting to be understood.

"B Corp is on the other side," said Natasha, as if reading off an autocue.

"The other side of what?" Hugh was starting to lose his temper. "The other side of the computer? We're in reality here. I really exist. You don't."

He wanted to set the record straight.

Peowww! A beam from the eraser-laser hit him in the shoulder. "Ouch!" he bellowed, raising a hand to a fresh wound.

Natasha was watching him. Slowly, ever so slowly, a smile lit up her impassive face. What kind of being *was* she?

"Natasha," he whispered. Tears of pain welled up in his eyes. The burning sensation was much sharper than the first time, as if everything was getting more intense. A tear rolled down his cheek.

Intrigued, Natasha moved closer, attracted by the water. She lifted her hand.

"No," begged Hugh. He was torn between terror and desire. He wanted her to touch him. He wanted to know. Would she have the same effect on him as Joke?

Natasha put her hand on his wet cheek. Hugh felt like a grenade had exploded inside his head, and was flung back against the wall.

The first thing he noticed when he regained consciousness was that Natasha had vanished into thin air. He heard the rattle of the typewriter and a message appeared on his screen:

Golem Natasha
size: to scale
mobility: good
vision: good
feeling: average
materialization: good
defence: average
invincible armour: inoperative
number of lives remaining: 3

Calimero cussed his computer.

When Hugh closed the door behind his strange girlfriend, Mrs Mullins wondered about calling the police. Then she decided the young, er, woman must be in fancy dress or taking part in one of those role-play things where you dress up as your hero. She liked this last idea because she remembered the message signed by Natasha: *Play with me. I'm waiting for you!* In short, having found an explanation, Mrs Mullins went to get supper ready.

Usually her kitchen was a space to unwind in. But she couldn't relax this evening. Not even peeling carrots, which she normally found therapeutic, did the trick. Was it knowing that Natasha was in Hugh's study, or – even worse – in his bedroom? She tried to calm down. Natasha was an impressionable young woman tormented by warrior fantasies. The weapon slung across her back bore no resemblance to a real one. It was a toy. Of course it was.

Bending over to get a bottle of olive oil out of the cupboard, she realized why she felt like she was suffocating. It was that smell again! She wrinkled up her nose. It was the same smell she'd noticed in

Hugh's study, a cross between sulphur and something burning. She was about to stand up again when she spotted the creepy-crawly hiding behind a jar of gherkins. She let out a shriek and dropped the oil.

Bubble flattened himself in the hope of escaping the boss. But she grabbed the weapon with stiff fur on the end and began pushing it in his direction.

"Pssst! Go on, shove off!"

Bubble unfolded his little wings and flapped over the oil slick.

"Hugh!" she called out, still wielding her broom. "Go on, pssst!"

Bubble spotted what seemed like a hideout in the graphics and disappeared into a black hole. Mrs Mullins gave a victorious bellow and closed the microwave door. Then, without really thinking, she turned it on.

"Hugh!" she screamed.

Hugh was still recovering from his brush with the seriously electric Natasha. "What is it now?" He ran into the kitchen and saw the microwave sparking furiously. His mother looked like she was waiting for it to take off.

"No!" she called out to her son. "Keep away, it's going to explode!"

But Hugh was past caring. He threw himself at the machine and switched it off. The door swung open and he saw what had been cooking.

"Bubble..."

"You know what it is?"

"Why are you microwaving him?"

Mother and son exchanged a look of disbelief for one of reproach.

"Close the door," Mrs Mullins sighed. "Or it'll escape."

"Escape?"

For a moment, Hugh mistook the microwaved Bubble for a plastic toy. But the door was still open and a current of air tickled the dragon's nostrils. Bubble let out a little ffmm, something between a splutter and a sneeze. Hugh pushed the door shut with both hands, leaning against it with all his weight. Things were getting out of hand. First Joke, then Natasha, and now Bubble. He turned to face his mother.

"Er, yes!" he said vaguely. "I forgot to tell you. I confiscated this, um, Sumatran dragon from one of my students. He'd brought it into class. You know him, actually: Samir Ben Azet. There's quite a trade in exotic animals on some estates these days."

Hardly able to believe her ears, Mrs Mullins repeated one word then another: *dragon, Ben Azet...*

"They tame anything from trapdoor spiders to boa constrictors and sell them to collectors. It's illegal, of course. What we've got here is an extremely rare kind of lizard."

"But it's got wings," Mrs Mullins murmured weakly.

"That's what makes it so rare. There are only twenty left in the world. It's a protected species." Then Hugh casually added, "By the way, can you remind me to call the zoo tomorrow?"

He was about to leave the kitchen when his mother called him back. "We can't leave it in the microwave!"

"D'you need to heat something up? Listen, I'm going to buy him a cage. Whatever you do, don't touch him, OK? Leave him right where he is."

"But, Hugh," implored Mrs Mullins, "he'll die of asphyxiation."

"No, he won't," he insisted. "Sumatran dragons have a small air pocket under their necks. A bit like an oxygen bottle. They're most unusual creatures." He headed back to the door, then turned round. "Whatever you do, don't touch him. When he's frightened, he spits a kind of poison." He smiled at his mother and said again, "Most unusual." Recent events had changed him. Totally. He was on another planet.

"By the way," he said, like an absent-minded teenager, "Natasha's sorry she couldn't say good-bye. She had to leave in a hurry…"

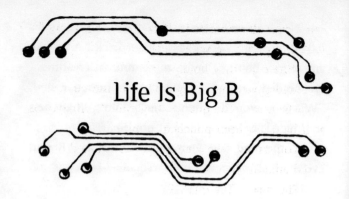

Life Is Big B

For once, Majid couldn't wait to get to school. He couldn't wait to tell Hugh about his big brother Haziz organizing the BIT Arena. It would bring glory to the Badach family for generations to come.

In the playground, Majid ran into a beaming Mamadou.

"Our English teacher's disappeared. We've got two free periods."

Majid scowled. Who was he going to share his good news with?

"Samir! Oi, Samir, guess what?"

Samir took a step back. He was suspicious of that question now. But when he heard the news, he came over all enthusiastic. "BIT Arena. Na-aa-ng!"

Majid puffed up with pride.

"Where are they holding it?"

Majid gave Samir a big smile. "In the quarry."

"The qua… The qua…" *The quarry?* Samir looked as if he'd just been punched in the gut.

"You know, the one that's abandoned," said Majid anxiously.

"The qua… The qua…"

Catastrophe.

After school, Samir and Majid rushed over to the quarry, Samir running and whinging at the same time.

"On the Koran's head, your brother's got some weird ideas. Joke at a games tournament! Are there gonna be nuff heads there?"

"A hundred, two hundred, dunno… But it's not Haziz's fault! If I'd known you'd moved Joke…"

They slowed down as they reached the first banner: *Welcome to the BIT Arena!* Others proclaimed: *Life is Big B.* Workmen were busy putting up a huge army tent where the players could sleep over.

"Aargh, man. We're done for," whispered Samir.

They couldn't even come back to find Joke after dark. A lorry had already delivered the amplifiers, PCs and cables, and two security guards from Big B Stores were patrolling the perimeter with a Rottweiler.

The manager of Big B Stores, Bernard Martin-Webber, could hardly contain himself. His idea for a sponsored games tournament was a master stroke. He'd alerted the press and invited the mayor. B Corp had analysed his store. Most of its consumers were young, so he needed to appeal to the youth of today. Bernard Martin-Webber (BMW for short) had swapped his pinstripe for jeans and trainers. He'd put on a black T-shirt with the slogan *Life is Big B* on it, and he was preening himself in the mirror.

"What d'you think?" he asked his mistress, who was lying on the sofa behind him. "Should I wear the baseball cap or not?"

His wife had already advised him against the idea. But two opinions were better than one.

"Couldn't care less," replied the young lady in question, chewing the skin around her fingernails.

"I'll wear it," decided BMW. "And what about the peak? Behind or to the side?"

"Like I said, who cares?"

"Behind. Great."

BMW admired his reflection for a moment. No two ways about it, it made him look younger.

The BIT Arena was supposed to start at 2 p.m. Haziz had hired Miloud and Rachid, Samir's cousins, as bouncers on the gate.

"Just make sure you only let guys through wearing the Big B T-shirt," he warned them.

"What's that about?" asked Miloud, sounding friendly enough.

"The T-shirt means they've paid the entry fee."

The cousins smirked and Rachid elbowed Haziz in the ribs. "Just so as we're clear our crew ain't paying."

Haziz frowned and jerked his head towards the security guards with the Rottweiler. "Sort it out with them," he said, walking off.

Maybe hiring Samir's cousins hadn't been such a great idea after all.

The gamers were starting to arrive and unload their gear. They gathered in their different teams: the Techno-Heads, the Goofys, the Moreland Masters. The insults were already flying.

"Hey, Spam, you lousy cheat, so you think you're gonna ghost again?"

"I'm gonna wipe the floor with you, Mickey. You won't know what's hit you!"

The computers had been installed on trestle tables in the largest excavated area of the quarry. Dozens of screens twinkled in the gloom and mounds of cables littered the floor like tangled spaghetti. A Big B Stores podium had just been set up and, even though the first Counter-Strike duels weren't due to start yet, BMW decided to warm things up. He stood in the spotlight, grabbed a mike and thundered:

"On behalf of Big B Stores, I am delighted to welcome you to the BIT Arena! Two days of non-stop competition. And with Big B cola and Mega B pizzas providing on-site refreshments, you don't even need to leave the premises. Don't forget to come and visit us at our stand. You'll find the latest in BIT technology from video games to computers, plus you'll walk away with a free souvenir tub of farting goo!"

Crouched down by one of the tables, Haziz was plugging in the last batch of computers. He stood up slowly, his face glowing with embarrassment. The gamers couldn't believe their ears. BMW, his baseball cap on back to front, in that bubblegum supermarket voice of his, was singing the praises of his bigger and better Big B Stores, a new and improved Big B Stores fit for Moreland Town!

"What d'you think you are? A comic or something?" Spam shouted. "You're not gonna bug us all weekend, man?"

Majid had just entered the main dugout wearing an expression as black as his T-shirt. If he'd been feeling his normal self, he'd have headed straight for the computers, or even the souvenir farting goo. But right now, all he could think about was that they'd have to force Joke to retreat into the depths of the quarry. The electric ectoplasm (as Sebastian still insisted on calling him) might be happy to stay where he'd been put, but the danger was that he'd be attracted to all the electricity in the BIT Arena.

"From Special B cereal to B Sporty BMXs, from a

New Generation BIT mobile phone to a top-of-the-range BIT games console," sang BMW as he went on, "you'll find everything you want at Big B Stores. Because life really is Big B!"

The mike was switched to max, allowing BMW to jabber away oblivious to the comments flying round the arena.

"Who is that loser? When's he going to stop killing our eardrums?"

"Hey, Haziz, can you pull the plug on that moron? Or I'll smash his face in."

While BMW was making a fool of himself, more and more friends of Mr Freebie were pouring through the main entrance. Samir's cousins weren't screening anybody, they just knocked fists and went "Safe, blud!" with their crew. It was like getting your hand stamped at a club. At first the security guards from Big B Stores tried to intervene, but a few knives casually pointed their way persuaded them to take Mirza the Rottweiler for a pee. Samir and Lulu got in just by smiling at Rachid.

"You're not going to tell them about Joke?" Lulu whispered to her big brother.

"No, Joke's our business and nobody else's."

Samir didn't know why, but he was convinced anybody over thirteen would be hostile towards Joke. His plan was to send Lulu to find the monster, and keep him calm. She'd got supplies for a romantic meal for two: batteries and a bar of Yummy B chocolate. It should be enough, since Joke had recently had a blowout dinner at the expense of Moreland Electricity.

"Farting goo! Fabby-dabby farting goo!" BMW crooned. "Of course, you're already collecting those tubs, but have you heard about our latest range?"

To the great surprise of sociologists and journalists, the farting goo trend was still going strong after several months.

"It's fluorescent, it shines in the dark, and it's currently on special offer. Buy two and get the cheapest one free!" cooed BMW into the microphone. "And now, here's just what you've been waiting for, young ladies, farting goo that's sparkly…" Apart from Lulu there wasn't a single girl in the BIT Arena, but BMW insisted on talking as if he was in the bargain section of Big B Stores. "We've got FG tubs to suit all purses and tastes," he added, deaf to Spam's sarcasm.

"What about the hallucinogenic one? You been snorting it?"

Everybody sniggered as the guys from Cyberstation tried to find a way to kill the sound without pulling the plug on the PCs.

"Go on," whispered Samir, pushing his little sister towards one of the tunnels.

A token red ribbon barred the way, but Lulu slipped underneath. She took a few steps in the dark before switching on her B Power torch. She knew how to reach Joke and, as she headed off, she could hear the reassuring sounds of the tournament in the background. Was she scared? Maybe, just a bit. It was very dark in the tunnel, and the beam of her torch jerked nervously from left to right.

After a hundred metres she called out, "Joke, are you there?" She crossed a cave, and then turned into a second tunnel.

"Joke, are you there?"

"Yippee-yay! It's pa-aa-arty time!" came her favourite voice.

Joke hadn't budged an inch. All big and swollen, he was giving off a blue-white light. Lulu rushed over and buried her face in his bouncy belly. As soon as they touched, waves of heat and energy rippled through her body. And something human got under Joke's skin too.

"Me friend," he said.

"I'm your first girlfriend," said Lulu, sounding very serious for a sick little girl. "And you're my first boyfriend."

"Friend," repeated Joke. "Cock-a-doodle-doo! The sun's come out to play!"

"Now you're talking rubbish," Lulu scolded. "You've got to think before you speak. You've got to think with your heart."

"Me got munchies," answered the monster in his Furby voice.

Lulu sighed and fished the batteries out of her backpack. Joke was insatiable. The more he ate, the more he wanted to eat.

"Yum, yum! Me still got munchies."

Lulu shrugged and took a bite out of each corner of her Yummy B chocolate bar. She didn't really understand why they had to hide Joke. Why couldn't they just move him into her bedroom? While she was reflecting sadly on how stupid grown-ups could be, Lulu didn't notice Joke getting increasingly excited. He couldn't resist the pull of the BIT Arena.

Back in the main dugout, BMW had at last handed over the mike to Haziz, who was busy reminding everybody about the rules for a clean Counter-Strike competition: no camping (waiting in ambush at strategic points) or ghosting (giving tips to your team once you were killed). Majid had found Samir, and the two of them were talking in hushed voices.

"Your sister's not going to spend two whole days with Joke, is she?"

"You got a better idea?"

"Won't your parents flip?"

Samir laughed darkly. "They start drinking Friday afternoon, and they're out of it all weekend."

Majid was watching the first on-screen duels while Samir was keeping an eye on his cousins. Miloud and Rachid were going from monitor to monitor, offering pills to the gamers.

"Anybody with a migraine?" asked Rachid. "I've got some mega-dose aspirin here."

"Those guys are losers!" Spam complained. He stood up and shouted, "Stop trying to contaminate our tournament. We don't want any of your drugs here!"

Miloud went over to him. "Shut it, or I'll fix your face so not even your old lady'll wanna look at it any more."

One of the players from Spam's team grabbed his arm and made him sit back down again.

"They're gonna trash the whole thing," Spam muttered, before replacing his headphones and turning back to his screen.

The cousins carried on touting for business. Mickey (from the Techno-Heads) succumbed. He'd never dropped an E before.

"It's like skunk but better," Rachid assured him.

Half an hour later, Mickey wasn't feeling anything, apart from a strong urge to empty his bladder. He left the main arena and nipped discreetly into a tunnel, ducking under a red ribbon. He wandered along for several metres. Instead of the way getting darker, he noticed a peaceful blue-white light guiding him. Maybe the organizers had installed proper toilets down there. Mickey carried on – and got the shock of his life. In front of him was a giant luminous creature, with gashes where its eyes and mouth should have been.

Mickey staggered and put a hand to his head. "Now I'm buzzing!"

Forgetting all about his call of nature, he hurried back to the arena. He didn't dare say anything to the other guys, and sneaked off to get some fresh air.

The manager of Big B Stores was looking for the mayor in the crowd. The press had arrived and BMW was determined to be photographed shaking hands with the local dignitary. But twenty minutes had already gone by and he still hadn't found the mayor. The photographer was getting impatient.

"Why don't I just take your photo inside?" he suggested.

BMW sighed and went back into the main arena, weighing up the big question: with or without the cap? Inside, he found something he hadn't bargained for. Joke was standing at the entrance to a tunnel, like a big luminous lump. Lulu was desperately trying to make him retreat.

"Me got munchies," Joke kept saying stupidly.

Those gamers who weren't totally hooked had let their eyes wander from the screen. They were watching the monster with amused smiles on their faces, convinced it was part of the entertainment. They all recognized the blob-shaped golem from the game.

"They're doing my head in with all their advertising gimmicks," grumbled Spam, who'd just been beaten nine–two.

The photographer, on the other hand, was delighted. "I'll take your photo with the beastie," he said to BMW. "Shake his hand instead. He's much more photogenic than the mayor."

"With or without the cap?" BMW wanted to know.

"With! It makes you look younger."

BMW quickly took it off. He always suspected the worst of everybody, especially if flattery was involved. He walked confidently over to Joke, hand held out.

Majid and Samir watched, frozen to the spot.

"We're going to take a photo," BMW said to the monster, thinking there was somebody inside. "Can you give me your hand – I mean your paw!"

Samir wanted to shout out "No, don't touch him!" But it was too late.

BMW felt like he'd been struck by lightning. His bones crackled, his brain exploded in a shower of sparks and he was hurled against a trestle table, upsetting players and computers. "It's electric! It's electric!" he shouted, his eyes nearly popping out of his head.

His panic was so obvious that nobody said anything for a moment. They were scared too.

"He's high on FG!" bellowed Samir, thinking fast. "Lulu, shake the nice gentleman's hand!"

Lulu slipped her tiny hand into Joke's huge paw and smiled at her captive audience. This reassured the gamers, who started hurling abuse at the unfortunate BMW.

"Stop pummelling FG," Spam advised him.

Still in shock, the manager wiped himself down with his cap and staggered over to the exit. Miloud, always ready for a laugh, decided it was his turn next and went over to Joke.

"Hey, Blobby, aren't you hot under all that? You gonna answer me, Mr Monster, or you want me to pump you down?"

"You mustn't call him monster," Lulu warned.

"How come you're standing up? Aren't you

meant to be dying of a genetic disease?" Miloud said tactfully.

Had Joke guessed Miloud wasn't a friend? Or was he acquiring a taste for giving shocks? Either way, he held out his paw to Miloud, saying, "Cock-a-doodle-doo! The sun's come out to play!"

Miloud held out his hand too, and Samir shut his eyes, muttering, "Aargh, man. I don't believe this…"

Same action, same effect: Miloud was catapulted three metres. He landed on a pile of cables. "It's electric! It's electric!" he shouted.

Everybody thought they were watching a planned sketch, and burst out laughing.

Miloud, half crazed with pain and terror, scrambled away on all fours, then spotted Rachid. "Let's get out of here!" he yelled. "It's electric! It's electric!"

Rachid couldn't get any sense out of him, so he led him off to get help. Meanwhile, Lulu had managed to coax Joke back down to the bottom of the tunnel by promising him more B Power batteries. Which meant things could get back to normal in the arena, without BMW and without the cousins, much to the great satisfaction of Spam (from the Fakers).

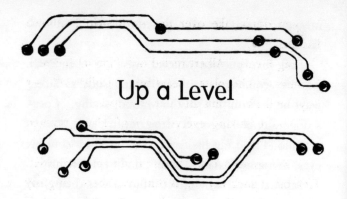

Up a Level

Nadia decided to keep Albert confined to the cramped space of her kitchen. If she let him feel at home and he thought there was the slightest chance of moving in, he'd jump at it. And that might not be all he jumped at.

"You're getting carried away!" she protested. "The way you're talking, anybody would think the Big B Corporation owned half the planet."

"That's their aim," replied Albert. "Right now, they own a quarter of it."

Nadia clinked her coffee spoon nervously against her cup. "Look, we're talking about sweets and gizmos. Yummy B marshmallows, farting goo

… you don't take over the world with wubbish like that."

"Big B cola," Albert reeled off, "Special B cereal, Yummy B chocolate, Beautiful B Dolly and her boyfriend Fit B, plus all their accessories."

"You're mixing everything up," Nadia pointed out.

"OK, so let's take things in the proper order. First off, I suck my Big B dummy. Then I hug my Big B Teddy. Then I brush my Beautiful B's hair and give Fit B his first suit. Seeing as I need to learn a thing or two, every so often I stick my nose in my B Smart storybooks. All of which works up a healthy appetite for… Well, I won't bore you with the full range of food, but we're talking hundreds of products. Yummy B sweets, Scrummy B ice creams… None of which make you fat, of course, and they're all great for your teeth. Luckily there's Mega B pizza, so I've got the strength to ride my B Sporty BMX—"

"Stop! That's enough!"

"Enough? It's never enough. We've still only conquered a quarter of the planet. And not just any old quarter."

Albert suddenly went quiet. The only sound in the kitchen was the plop of water from the tap into the stainless-steel sink.

"Have you noticed something?" he asked.

"What?"

"The quarter I'm telling you about consists largely of kids under fifteen."

"No!" Nadia let out a tiny cry of despair.

"Millions and millions of consumers," Albert continued. "And when we've got them, Nadia, we've got the world. Because we're there, waiting for them at the crossroads. We're with them all the way. Personal stereos, video games, mobile phones, PCs. We sell those too. And later on it's washing powder, sofas, air pistols—"

"Stop!"

"We sell everything. From the first teat on baby's bottle to granny's wheelchair. From my Big B dummy in the cradle to my Big Hole in the graveyard—"

"Albert!" she pleaded, blocking her ears.

He picked up the coffee pot and poured a stream of steaming liquid into his cup. A satisfied smile hovered on his lips.

"Albert?"

"Yes?"

Nadia was looking at him with a mixture of anger and fear. "Why d'you keep saying *we*?"

"I said *we*?"

"When you're talking about them, you say *we*."

He seemed to be looking for the answer in the bottom of his cup. "All right, I'll come clean," he said gruffly. "I was one of them. And that's how they teach you to think. Eat Big B, work Big B. *Life is Big B*. But I'll get them, Nadia, I swear I'll get them."

"You? Albert against a quarter of the planet!"

"No. Us."

Nadia's face twitched.

"You and me, Nadia. Us."

"Oh…"

Albert emptied the coffee pot and put some more water on to boil. He desperately needed to talk. So Nadia listened. According to him, the tiniest tub of farting goo was a threat and every cereal packet was a deadly trap. And behind all of this loomed the grotesque figure of an obese dwarf called Mr William.

Mr William was insatiable. Mr William swallowed whole chunks of the market like you swallow a piece of cake. Mr William was an ogre who devoured little children. And that was just for starters.

"But at the end of the day, we're free to choose," Nadia protested. "So why do kids all want the same thing at the same time, the same tubs of that revolting goo, the same T-shirt? The same CD by the same singer."

"Because *we're* talking to them, because *we're* telling them it's good for them. Sorry, I'm getting worked up again." He lowered his voice and added, "That's what I found out one day. And that's why I left."

"What? What did you find out?"

"That Big B was camping in my game, to use the kids' terminology."

And Albert told her all about being a brilliant but naive young IT wizard, who spent his days and nights programming a mega-buff game, an ultra-grimy game, a scary-trashy game. Golem. But who asked no questions.

"One day I started noticing a few suspicious

signs. Like shadows, evil echoes behind my beautiful designs. You see, while I was busy developing my graphics, my characters, they were playing a different tune. Secret messages, subliminal images. Almost undetectable. You think you're on the dragon's back visiting Golemia? Actually you're being brainwashed: BUY BIG B FARTING GOO!"

Nadia jumped. Albert had shouted the slogan.

"What could I do? Destroy everything? I was working in a fortress, under constant surveillance from cameras and security guards. Leave? Yeah, I wanted to leave, all right. But nobody walks out on B Corp. B Corp walks out on you. And mostly it's goodbye for ever. A one-way ticket to your Big Hole."

"But you managed to get out."

Albert clasped his fingers together and cracked his knuckles.

"Yes. The day of the big bug. Every floor was disabled. There was smoke in the corridors and people running in every direction. All the systems had crashed. Electric locks, radars, video circuits. Mr William requisitioned half the guards for his personal protection, to form a human shield. He feared an assassination attempt. I got out. More importantly, I got my computer out too. With my game inside it."

He sounded proud, even slightly conceited.

"And now they're after me. There are thousands of them, they've got billions in the bank, and they're after me. Because they know that if anybody can topple them, I can."

"Of course you can. And might I ask how?"

Albert suddenly grabbed her hand under the little kitchen table. "First of all," he said, "I have to find somewhere to stay."

Nadia snatched her hand away. "Oh, tewiffic. My hero's looking for a nice girl who'll stay at home to keep his meals hot and his bed warm. Sorry, Albert, but you've messed up on the casting."

"Nadia, you've misunderstood me!"

"I've misunderstood you? Well, that's one way of putting it! Let me tell you what I think, shall I? I think you've got a serious nerve!"

Albert looked offended. But Nadia was just getting going.

"You were working away at your innocent little game with its sweet little monsters, where you score points every time there's a bloodbath. You were teaching the youth of today they've got to massacre everybody if they want to get to the next level. And all this in a bunker guarded by an army of killers hired by some psychopath who wants to gobble up half the planet…"

Nadia caught her breath before spitting out, "And you didn't smell a rat?"

From the way Albert stiffened, she could tell she'd hit a nerve.

"You're very harsh," he grumbled. "OK, so I was blind. Creating a computer game is incredibly exciting, you know, but yeah, it doesn't always help you to see things for what they are. For two years I only saw what I wanted to see. Brilliant job, great salary—"

"I've got a brilliant job too," Nadia interrupted. "Shame about the salary. But I'll tell you something: it's much tougher getting the kids to go up a level at Moreland School than it is in Golemia."

Albert shook his head, as if acknowledging defeat. But she knew he wasn't finished.

"You can't back out of this," he said coldly. "Your fate's linked with mine from now on. They know who you are and where you are. If they want to get me, they'll go through you. And they do want to get me."

There was genuine terror in Nadia's eyes now. "What are you saying?"

"If I stick close to you, you'll be in danger. But I'll be there to protect you. If I go away, they'll get you. And they'll do whatever it takes to make you talk. Even if you don't know anything."

"You—" She stood up so abruptly her chair tipped backwards onto the tiled floor. Then she stormed out of the kitchen like a Fury.

Albert heard things falling over, doors being slammed, drawers squeaking. Moments later she was back, her arms full. She threw the whole lot on the floor: two big flat cushions, a pillow and a blanket.

"You can sleep between the bin and the fridge," she told him. "Next door is my space. I don't want you in it."

"But, Nadia—"

"I get up at seven o'clock. I eat my bweakfast at quarter past. I expect you to be up by then with everything tidied away. And I expect you to be out.

First thing in the morning, my eyes are puffy and my skin looks kind of gween. No way am I letting a man watch me eating toast when I've got my witch's head on. Is that clear?"

There was a long silence, and then Nadia burst out laughing. "You can close your mouth now."

"Nadia, sweetheart…"

"Huh?"

"I'll be up a level before you know it."

Which was how Albert came to stay at Nadia's without really moving in. The kitchen and the tiny entrance hall were the only rooms in the Voltaire Street flat he was allowed in. Till Nadia relented and let him use the bathroom too. He spent most of his waking hours out and came back in the evenings after grabbing a lonely bite to eat.

On the third evening, he found Nadia in his territory. In the kitchen. The science teacher was up to something. She had test tubes, flasks, sachets of powder and an old-fashioned pair of weighing scales, with every size of weight to go with it, spread all over the table. When Albert walked in, she barely looked up.

"I see you've brought some work home with you," he said in a conversational tone.

Nadia grunted.

"I know you get a lot of marking, but you didn't tell me about this," he went on. "I didn't realize science teachers played at being chemists in their kitchens."

Nadia glanced at him and then started counting drops from her glass pipette into a flask.

"What kind of experiment is it? Nothing dangerous, I hope."

"Enough to blow up the planet."

"Help!" he exclaimed and started laughing. "No wonder people talk about estates being dangerous, if this is what kids learn at school these days."

Nadia corked the flask and gave it a good shake. "What I'm working on has nothing to do with school. But you're wight, it's got a lot to do with not feeling safe. I don't feel safe. So guess what? I've decided to pwotect myself."

"From who?"

"From my enemies, my friends, the whole world. If a man ever got it into his head to attack me in the middle of the night, for example, I'd be ready to counter-attack. A good squirt of vitriol works wonders."

"This is becoming an obsession!" he protested. "Why d'you want to dissolve me at all costs?"

"Hey, you wecognized yourself!"

"Nadia, I swear… Nadia?"

The science teacher had put her head in her hands and her shoulders shook with silent sobs. "I'm scared, Albert. I've seen them. They're watching me. They're following me."

"Who? When?"

"The van with the satellite dish." Nadia stood up and wiped her eyes with her sleeve. "I'm scared every time I set foot outside. I'm scared to go anywhere any more. I stick close to other people when I'm in the street. So I've decided to protect myself."

Albert looked incredulously at the flasks and sachets.

"Trust me, when you know a thing or two about chemical weactions, you can do some serious damage," she assured him.

"That's what I'm worried about. But why won't you agree to my suggestion?"

Albert spent over an hour trying to convince

Nadia that she should let him be responsible for her protection. Let him escort her when she went out, like a bodyguard. But she refused indignantly.

"Great! You'll put two Yummy B chocolate biscuits in my satchel and give me a peck on the cheek in front of the school gates."

Albert tried again. "You don't know who you're dealing with, Nadia. We're talking about professional killers here, specialists in electronic tracking techniques. D'you really think you're going to scare them off with your fairy dust?"

"Well, lend me your gun then, if that'd make you feel better. I'm a good shot – I always hit the ducks at the fair."

He sighed. "OK, listen up. Starting from tomorrow, whether you like it or not, I'm going to keep an eye on you when you're out and about. Don't worry, I'll keep my distance. You won't even see me. But I'll be there, ready to intervene if necessary."

Nadia went bright red. "D'you think I'm a complete idiot? I know perfectly well that's what you've been doing for the past few days. But he was still there, wasn't he, that fatso in his van!"

"All right, all right. At least it's out in the open now. Come on, it's late. I've got a date with the bin and the fridge." Albert jerked his chin towards the table covered in chemicals. "And thanks for getting my breakfast ready."

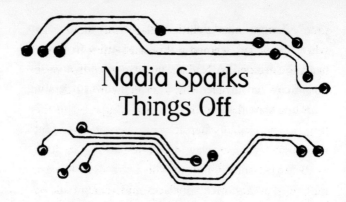

Nadia Sparks
Things Off

The funny thing was, ever since Albert had turned her life upside down, Nadia's timetable had become as regular as clockwork. No detours, no stop-offs. She rushed from Voltaire Street to Moreland School and back again, always following the same route and always using the busiest streets.

At four o'clock on this particular afternoon, however, she changed her routine. She knew she was taking a risk, a big risk, but she was doing somebody a favour. Instead of going home via the main roads, she made for the old town: a few blocks of red-brick houses huddled around a church blackened by the years. It was a hangover from the time when it was a little village surrounded by wheat fields and seemed a thousand miles from the heaving metropolis. Nadia's grandmother had been born there, in a house with a wrought-iron balcony.

Nadia would have liked to stop and stroll in the tiny square with its heroic white rose bushes. But she carried on her way, without pausing to look in the sweet-shop window where she used to gaze longingly at liquorice shoelaces and marshmallows as a little girl. In the good old days, when every sweet in the world wasn't stamped with the Yummy B logo.

She had just turned down a narrow, deserted street. She heard him before she saw him. The trap was working, but who would be the victim? She walked calmly on for a few more metres, fighting the urge to run for her life. At last she allowed herself a quick glance over her shoulder. He was there all right. The van, with its blacked-out windows and satellite dish, was trailing slowly behind her.

This time, Nadia picked up the pace. And the van accelerated. She knew the old town like the back of her hand, and she knew she had to reach the end of the little street first. She started running.

Nothing looked less like a refuge than the back of St Guinevere's Church. A dead zone surrounded by high walls, it stank and was littered with empty crates. The locals avoided it, even in broad daylight. Nadia kept checking to see what was happening behind her as she crossed it. When the van turned into the back alley, she was only twenty metres ahead.

Her pursuer was taking his time now, thinking he'd got her.

She ducked under a narrow moss-covered archway made of black stones. The van wouldn't be able to get through, and straight after the arch came the steps. Nadia knew exactly how many there were – fourteen – like she knew each crack. As a little girl she'd hopped up and down them a thousand times, keeping to the dark joins or the pale spots... Today she was playing a different game. She tore down the steps three at a time.

She heard the van braking and the door slam.

At the bottom of the steps she turned round. The person chasing her was standing under the archway. Nadia thought she saw him smile. He was greasy and heavy. She was sure *he'd* never competed in the regional one hundred metres sprint final. Go for it! In her mind she wedged her running shoes into the starting blocks. Eyes straight ahead. *Bang!* Nadia shot off as if the starting gun had just been fired. She silently urged herself on. Go for it, girl, you're faster than that fatso.

At the corner of St Guinevere's Square, somebody was following her progress through a tiny pair of opera glasses. Somebody who felt bad about making her take such a risk. Albert had been amazed Nadia had agreed to the idea, and undertaken it so readily.

She was heading for a dirt path now, with small allotments on either side. Her grandmother used to grow leeks there. Out of the corner of her eye she could see bamboo canes with tomato plants growing up them, just a short distance from the Moreland Estate. It was a miracle. And Nadia suddenly felt she was fighting for them, for these allotments.

B Corp won't get them! a voice shouted inside her head.

Three hundred metres of land sloped gently downwards. Wooden gates, leaves, fruits and warm odours. Eddie, short of breath, was making the earth tremble with his clumsy pounding.

Clasping his binoculars, Albert urged Nadia on. She ran like a queen, with long easy strides, back straight. Her blonde hair crowned her head. The guy behind was losing ground with every step.

A main road ran along the bottom of the allotments. And her clapped-out old scooter was waiting at the foot of the big beech tree. Nadia prayed it would start first go.

Albert held his breath. Nadia had just disappeared in the shadow of the beech tree. Three or four long seconds went by. The scooter's engine creaked, then spluttered into life.

Go on, go on, Albert willed it.

At last he saw what he'd been waiting for. Nadia was accelerating away, leaving her pursuer doubled over by the side of the road.

Albert was bowled over. "What a champion!" he shouted. Then he rushed over to the van.

The back of the vehicle was what interested him most, because that was where the technician kept his detecting equipment. He tried the handle. No luck. The guy wasn't that stupid. The doors were seriously reinforced. For a brief moment, Albert thought about shooting the lock. There was nobody around, it was a quiet part of town...

He paused for a second, but decided to check first to see if Techno Kid hadn't made a fatal mistake when he tore off after Nadia. A quick glance told Albert that he hadn't. He cursed. No, the fat oaf hadn't forgotten to take the ignition key with him. What about the driver's door – had he locked that? Yes, of course. Techno Kid hadn't lost his head in the heat of the moment.

Albert knew he only had two or three minutes. He'd managed to separate the guy from his van. Now he had to take full advantage of the situation. Otherwise Nadia would have sprinted for nothing.

Then he spotted something. Over on the passenger side the window was open. He rushed round and climbed up onto the running board. He could fit his arm through the gap, but the door wouldn't open. There was something on the seat. A denim jacket. He grabbed it without bothering to search the pockets. He could do that later. Now he had to make his getaway.

Once again he felt like shooting. Puncturing a tyre, destroying the satellite dish. Instead he spat on the handsome white bodywork and slipped away.

"And that's what I wisked my life for?"

Nadia eyed the denim jacket, which was rolled up on the kitchen table.

"I was counting on you to make him lose his head, so he'd leave the key in the ignition," said Albert sheepishly. "There must have been loads of interesting gear in there."

"You overestimate me. I hope you got his cwedit card, ID and mobile, at least."

"I waited for you before going through it. But I already know we won't find anything. His pockets are as empty as mine."

Nadia shook the jacket out. Then she slid her hand into the right pocket. "Hold on. A box of matches!"

"Terrific."

She continued her methodical exploration, but all she found was a cheap biro and a piece of folded paper.

"I should have waited for him," growled Albert. "Bumped him off."

"Hang on, there's something written here."

"Don't tell me, the code to break into B Corp HQ."

"*Gwanter*," read Nadia. "D'you think that's fatso's name?"

"*Gwanter*? Hold on. Gwa... Granter!" exclaimed Albert, ripping the piece of paper out of Nadia's hands.

"Does it mean anything to you?"

"It's a common enough name, but I don't think it's a coincidence. There was a Granter at B Corp. A real high-flyer. A security systems analyst. The best."

A number was written under the name, starting with 07. A mobile number. On the other side was a sketch map.

"And he's left B Corp?" asked Nadia.

"Yes."

"I didn't think you could leave B Corp."

But Albert wasn't listening. He was examining the diagram, trying to decipher it.

"The A96 must be a road," he concluded, tracing a wiggly line with his finger. "And there's another: B702. And that's a cross. It's not looking good. I already told you what happens to people who desert our big happy family. I've got to warn him. As it happens, I wanted to talk to him anyway. If I could just get him on our side..."

He looked at his watch. "Have you got a road map?"

"Yes, boss. And then can I go to bed?"

The following morning, at exactly 7.15 a.m., Albert and Nadia were eating breakfast at the kitchen table.

"I got hold of Granter last night," said Albert. "He sounded worried. Apparently, that little cross marks a point on a journey he makes several times a week. A hundred miles south of where he lives. He's got a contract with a company, but he wouldn't give me their name. He was very suspicious, but I managed to persuade him to see me. We're meeting the day after tomorrow in the city."

"The day after tomorrow? I should be able to make it."

"To do what?"

"You're not going to leave me on my own, boss? There won't be anybody around to pwotect me," Nadia whimpered.

Albert looked sullen. She was winding him up.

"We're a team, aren't we?" she went on in a different tone of voice. "Or did I get it wrong? Nadia's only useful as the scapegoat to attract the big bad wolf."

"Why don't you just—"

"—put on my red cape and go round to Grandma's house?"

Albert shook his head, but he was smiling.

"Why are you looking at me like that?" Nadia asked.

"I was thinking you look quite cute when you're angry."

"I'll take that as a compliment." She dunked a buttered corner of toast in her coffee. Greasy drops formed on the surface. "Tell me, this Granter guy, are you sure about him?"

"I'm not sure about anything at the moment. To be honest, I hardly know him. But as you've pointed out, I can't fight B Corp on my own. If this guy left, there must be a reason. He's bound to be a threat to them."

"I hope you wecognized his voice?"

"Not sure of anything," Albert said again.

"What if it's a trap?" she asked.

"That's exactly why—"

"—we should go there together."

Albert couldn't stop staring at the two girls with their backs to him, perched on stools in the reddish glow of the bar. A skinny Afro-Caribbean in boots and a leather skirt, and a big blonde whose large bosom was threatening to burst out of her corset. They were sipping fruit juice while waiting for their clients.

"I should never have let you come," he told Nadia. "It's no place for a girl like you."

"He's got weird tastes, your friend Gwanter."

Albert lit a cigarette and checked out every centimetre of the small bar for the thirtieth time. He took in the poster advertising a bottle of champagne at some exorbitant price, the coat rack where a silver jacket and a transparent plastic mac were hanging up, the wilting plant. The black bars on the window. Grim.

The blonde opened her beaded handbag and started powdering her face again.

"He told me it was grotty," admitted Albert.

"You got your eye on the black girl or the blonde one?"

"It's nine o'clock. He should be here by now."

The door opened and a man walked in. He was young and weedy, with round glasses and a dark crew cut. He scanned the room, spotted Albert and Nadia, frowned, paused. He made his way over to them, keeping an eye on the bar.

"You're not alone," he whispered, looking disapprovingly at Nadia.

Albert stiffened. "And you're not Granter."

"Granter sent me. He didn't say anything about a second person."

"Who are you? I'm only prepared to talk to—"

"Granter wants me to take you to him," the man cut in. "He's got to be careful."

"Me too," replied Albert.

"My car's right outside the door."

Albert stared at his glass of sparkling mineral water. "I don't like this. Where are we going?"

"Not far. Ten minutes from here. I can't tell you any more than that."

"D'you want to blindfold us too? No, I don't like this at all. Can you get him on the phone?"

The man seemed to be expecting this question. He got out his mobile and pressed a button twice. Somebody picked up straight away.

"Granter? It's Mark. He wants to talk to you. OK, I'm passing him over." The young man held out the handset.

"This little trip wasn't part of the plan," Albert told the person on the other end. "I've got to be sure this isn't a lousy trap. Listen up, Granter. What's sixty-seven times thirty-eight?" He grinned. "OK. Two thousand five hundred and forty-six. Sounds right to me."

He handed the mobile back to the man called Mark. "Granter's a genius at mental arithmetic," he explained to Nadia. "Everybody knew how brilliant he was at B— back there. And I'm not bad at it either. All right, I think it's safe to go ahead with this."

"Is the young lady coming with us?" asked Mark.

"Of course I'm—"

Nadia broke off. Albert looked round. The big blonde had moved in on him. The barrel of a revolver was sticking out of her handbag.

"Of course she's coming with us," the big

blonde said in a voice that was unequivocally male.

Albert slid his fingers slowly down his jacket, searching for the weapon he could feel against his hip.

"Don't move!" ordered the blonde.

Mentally Albert undressed her. Removed her wavy wig, her false breasts, her fishnet tights and heavy make-up ... and what he found was the oafish guy from the van. His girlfriend was standing right behind him, cool as a cucumber. Albert had time to notice that she had a square jaw and hair on the back of her hands. Tucked safely behind the bar, the barman was absent-mindedly drying a glass.

Mark looked confused. The intervention had clearly taken him as much by surprise as it had Albert.

"You're going to leave quietly, in single file," declared Eddie, casually propping up his left breast. "This nice gentleman will drive us to Granter. Two birds with one stone, Mr Albert. I've got a feeling we're about to spend a fruitful evening together. Would you like to stand up?"

Albert glanced at Nadia. She was glued to her chair, clutching her canvas bag to her chest. "All right, I'll go with you," he said, "but little missy stays here. This has nothing to do with her."

Eddie grunted disapprovingly. "Sorry, Mr Albert, but I've done a lot of running after her. I'd hate to think I'd gone to all that trouble for nothing. If this has nothing to do with her, she shouldn't have got mixed up with it in the first place."

"Come on, let's go," ordered the skinny one with the hairy legs. "On your feet, everybody!"

Albert saw Mark glance desperately at the barman. But the guy had clearly been bribed to turn a blind eye. He'd been drying the same glass for a good few minutes now.

Just then, Nadia burst into tears and Eddie waved his gun at her. "Pull yourself together, miss. Nothing's going to happen to you, as long as Mr Albert cooperates."

Nadia sniffed noisily and groped around in her bag for a handkerchief.

"Stand up!" growled the sidekick with the burgeoning beard, sounding less and less like a woman. "We're leaving. Let's step on it!"

Nadia gave him an apologetic look. She dipped her handkerchief in Albert's glass and pulled it out again. She stood up, patting her cheeks, and took two steps towards the door.

"Your bag," said Eddie politely.

Nadia had left her canvas bag on the back of her chair. Eddie just had time to notice a strange plume of smoke coming from it, when it exploded. A great cloud of acrid smoke filled the room. Pressing her drenched handkerchief against her face, Nadia rushed towards the exit, grabbing Albert by the arm on her way out.

"Stop!" shouted Eddie. "Aarrghh.∴" He was choking, and so were Mark, Albert, the girlfriend with the deep voice and the barman.

Nadia pushed Albert outside, and he stumbled forward blindly. In the cool night air he opened his eyes again. Nadia started running, dragging him by the hand. Thirty metres away, they looked round. Mark and the two transvestites from B Corp had formed a curious trio on the pavement, surrounded by wreaths of smoke. Cars were braking and hooting in the street. Heads appeared at windows. People were rushing out of their houses.

"Let's go!" said Albert. "I don't think anything'll happen to Mark now."

They ran side by side for two or three minutes. Albert coughing. Nadia laughing. Then they dived into a doorway and, with their eyes still streaming and their throats still burning, they kissed.

"You're a dangerous lady," growled Albert eventually. "I'm not sleeping with your explosives any more!"

"I dare say we could come to another awangement," said Nadia in her sensible schoolteacher's voice.

But the look she gave Albert was enough to set anybody on fire.

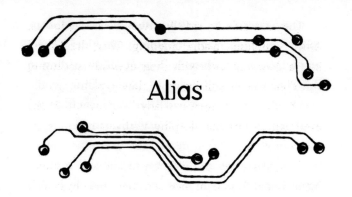

Alias

Hugh had a note from his doctor that said he needed time off work for depression. Day and night he sat slumped in front of his computer. Golem regularly popped up on his screen, but the young teacher couldn't bring himself to summon Natasha again. He'd managed to shut Bubble inside a crate and drill a few holes in it, because Mrs Mullins was worried about the poor beastie's health. In doing so, he'd accidentally brushed against the little dragon and received the kind of shock you get off an electric fence. Bubble seemed harmless enough. The little spark that came out of his mouth barely singed the wooden walls of his prison.

The eraser-laser, on the other hand, had done some serious damage to Hugh's shoulder. There was a burn mark where he'd been hit, extending in the kind of sharp incision a Stanley knife would make. The eraser-laser had burnt and cut through flesh. Hugh wondered if Natasha's virtual powers might become even more real the next time round.

After two days and two nights, he still couldn't bring himself to type *Alias*. Why should he bother with a girl who electrocuted him as soon as she touched him? When he was tired of gazing at her on his screen, he closed his eyes and saw a life-sized version of her imprinted on his eyelids. Life-sized, but not quite natural. The regularity of pixels and shading failed to recreate a real complexion, or the imperfections of human flesh. Natasha was other, *alias*, too beautiful to be true. But do I truly love her? wondered Hugh. Without realizing what he was doing, he typed the five letters. He was calling her back. Too bad if he died.

"Water is the weapon of B Corp," rattled off Natasha when she was standing in front of him once more. "I must not touch water."

Presumably she'd had another conditioning

session on the other side. But she hadn't forgotten her mission.

"I have come to destroy B Corp."

Peowww! A beam shot out of the eraser-laser and struck a BIT personal stereo.

"One hit," she whispered. She lowered her weapon abruptly to reload. *Peowww!* A can of Big B cola exploded.

"Reload."

"No, no!" roared Hugh. "Natasha, stop."

She pointed her weapon at him. He was next.

"Calimero is our ally," he pleaded.

"Calimero is our ally," she repeated, lowering the eraser-laser again. "I have come to destroy B Corp."

"You can't do that," Hugh told her.

How could he make her understand her mistake? She'd got B Corp and the real world muddled up. He carefully edged round her and walked over to the window. He opened the curtains to let in the sunlight and tapped on the glass. "The whole of reality," he said, "is on the other side."

Natasha followed him with her eyes, without moving. Was she getting the pane mixed up with the computer screen? Hugh opened the window.

Outside was the street. Shop displays, people, real life. Natasha didn't move. But she looked out of the window. At life.

"I cannot switch graphics yet," she protested. "I have not killed all the enemies on the first level."

"There are millions of levels, billions of levels," Hugh told her. "We're in the real world here. And it's infinite."

Natasha raised her weapon. She was going to fire. Where? At what? At who?

"Calimero is our ally!" shouted Hugh in desperation.

"Calimero is our ally, Calimero is our ally, Calimero is our ally, Calimero…"

Natasha fell silent. She was totally disorientated. She moved closer to the window. Her eyes were darting in every direction. Her mouth opened and closed but no sound came out. The breeze from outside ruffled her hair, flicking back the strands that covered her forehead. Hugh was horrified to see EMET, the word that gave life to the golem, branded on her flesh. He closed the window and drew the curtains again.

"Let's stay on the first level," he said gently.

He felt very sorry for Natasha. She wasn't a robot, but she wasn't a human either. She existed in her own way. *Another way.*

"Alias," he whispered.

"Alias is my master," she recited.

Hugh came up to her. Closer, closer still. The projection of all his desires was right under his nose. In spite of himself, he stretched out a hand to just a few millimetres away from Natasha's mouth, traced the outline of her shoulder in the air. Then he sighed and gave up.

"Calimero is our ally," she said.

"My name's Hugh, actually, and if you really existed I'd tell you I love you. I'd tell you…" He turned away, afraid he was going to start crying. His gaze fell on the wooden crate with Bubble inside.

"Of course!" Why not connect the two virtual beings? He lifted the lid a little and Bubble came into view, pale, almost transparent. He needed to recharge.

"The dragon!" Natasha cried out.

Automatically she took Bubble out of the box and he curled up in her arms, like a kitten. Hugh would have given anything to swap places with the miniature dragon. Within a few seconds Bubble had got his colour back, as if he recharged on coming into contact with another virtual being. His blue eyes had gone all gooey, and from the back of his throat came a gentle purr. *Merrr merrr...*

"Alias is looking for the dragon," said Natasha, sounding almost normal this time.

"Why?"

"He must not be on the other side. He is a bug."

Once more, Hugh had the extraordinary feeling that they were engaged in a dialogue which had never been programmed.

"So Alias didn't want to let the dragon out?"

"The dragon is a bug."

Who was Alias? Whatever its nature, whatever its powers, it was making some big mistakes. Maybe Joke was also a bug that had escaped Alias's control.

The phone rang in the sitting room. It was probably his mum. She knew he was off work sick, and she'd only worry if he didn't answer.

"I'm changing levels," he said as he moved away from Natasha. He closed the door behind him and ran over to the phone. "Yes? It's me, Mum! Yeah, don't worry, I'm fine."

Hugh wasn't fine at all. While he was talking to his mother, a revolting spectacle was taking place before his eyes: a virtual being was walking through the closed study door. Clusters of coloured pixels went through the barrier and tried to re-form again on the other side. There were two or three seconds of chaos, with the outlines of arms, eyes and legs being sketched in the air only to disappear again. Finally all the pixels got caught up in a whirlwind, as if they were being spun in a centrifuge. The result was the gorgeous cocktail otherwise known as Natasha.

Dazed, Hugh dropped the receiver. "Really, I'm fine," he mumbled.

"Watch out, behind you!" Natasha called out.

Peowww! The laser beam hit the goldfish bowl.

"Water is the weapon of B Corp," she said.

"That's enough!" shouted Hugh.

The bowl had exploded, and both unlucky goldfish were quivering on the carpet.

Reload. *Peowww!* Reload. *Peowww!*

"You … you've killed them," he stammered.

"How many points do I get?" Natasha enquired.

Appalled, he bent down to get a closer look at the fish. The laser beam had targeted their heads and incinerated them. It was horrifying. Hugh shuddered. Then he heard the sinister *click-clack* of the eraser-laser being reloaded.

"Don't fire any more," he begged. "There is no enemy here."

What madness had he been dragged into? He noticed the soaking wet carpet. There was still a chance of getting on top of the situation.

"Come here," he said to Natasha. "Come to me. Calimero is your ally."

Natasha took one step towards the trap and then, with the end of her eraser-laser, pointed to the carpet.

"Water."

She'd had that particular experience before and logged it. So she *was* able to memorize things, to analyse and make deductions. In short, she could adapt the way a human being would. What right did Hugh have to destroy her? The water pistol was still in his pocket. But firing it would be like murdering her.

"I don't know what to do any more," he said, half to himself and half out loud. The real and the virtual were becoming hopelessly mixed up.

"What did you do with Bubble?" The little dragon was no longer in Natasha's arms. Hugh panicked. "The dragon? Where's the dragon?"

"I left him on the first level," she answered. "He cannot walk through walls."

Hugh ran into his study. Unsurprisingly, Bubble had not gone back into his crate.

"Watch out, next to you!" Natasha warned him.

Peowww! Puff Z Sniddy erupted into smithereens.

"CALM DOWN, D'YOU HEAR? CALM DOWN!"

Hugh was at his wits' end. Without stopping to think, he lashed out at Natasha. Then, terrified, he pulled his hand back and looked at her in amazement. He'd only got a tiny shock. But there was no time to find out why. Natasha was pointing her eraser-laser at him. He had attacked her, so she had to defend herself.

"No! Calimero is your ally!"

But she was aiming at him. The words that had protected him up to now didn't seem to work any more.

"Don't kill me," he begged. "I've only got one life. I haven't lived yet, Natasha. I haven't even experienced love." He was crying.

"Hugh," she said, pronouncing his name harshly.

He was trembling from head to toe. "Have … have you understood?" he stammered. "Yes, that's it, my name's Hugh."

"And if you really existed I'd tell you I love you," Natasha recited flatly.

She'd registered his words. Hugh was astonished. Slowly, carefully, he stretched his hand towards her, pushed aside the eraser-laser, skimmed her hair, ran his fingers over her shoulder. Each gesture gave him a tiny shock. It wasn't particularly pleasant, but it didn't exactly hurt either.

"What would happen if I kissed you?" he wondered out loud. Then he shook his head. He had to find Bubble first. "Where's the dragon?"

"He is there," said Natasha, pointing to the antique chest of drawers.

Hugh bent down and spotted Bubble cowering under the furniture. "You, old thing, are going back in your kennel." He slid the crate along with his foot and grabbed a small plastic ruler off his desk. Then he lay down on his front.

Bubble squashed himself against the skirting board. He'd finally realized he was a pathetically small dragon with a useless jet of fire. And to think he'd once terrorized whole populations! Now he was terrified by the boss with the broom, and even Gangly Guy was persecuting him. They got him every time. This game sucked. Something rotten. In a fit of pique, Bubble shot out a little flaming *grrmffussh*.

"Cor! Scary!" teased Hugh. He put the wooden crate just in front of the dragon's muzzle and tickled his flank with the end of the ruler. "Pssst! Back in your box, sunshine."

Bubble tried to run away, but got whacked on the rump by the ruler. In the end he surrendered and shuffled sheepishly into the crate.

"Good boy!" crowed Hugh, putting on the lid. He'd almost forgotten Natasha was watching. What did she make of it all? He looked round nervously.

"The dragon must return to the other side," said Natasha.

"No, I'm keeping him," Hugh blurted out more quickly than he meant to. His heart was racing, the way it did every time he opposed Natasha. But she didn't point her weapon at him.

"Alias is looking for the dragon," she said, as if she wanted to discuss the matter.

"Alias is not my master." It wasn't exactly a declaration of war, but it *was* a declaration of independence. Calimero wasn't a guaranteed ally.

"Alias is my master," said Natasha. "Alias is... Alias..." She got stuck again.

Bubble was moving around inside his crate and squeaking. Was it because he could sense Natasha so close to him? Hugh raised the lid and saw the dragon's tiny head.

Merrr merrr...

Hugh smiled tenderly. "If you're a good dragon, Natasha will hold you again," he promised.

As he went to lower the lid, Bubble's head suddenly shot up. His blue eyes changed to red and he spat his jet of fire. He was fully recharged now and Hugh got a fright that made him step back. The jet was a real miniature flame. But it quickly went out and Hugh burst out laughing.

"Naughty dragon!" he exclaimed, putting the lid back down. Then he smiled at Natasha. "Bubble's great! My mother always refused to get me a dog, but anyway I prefer dragons now." He was genuinely happy. No reaction from the girl-golem. His smile quickly faded. Had she disconnected?

"Are you still there? Hey, darling?" He put his hands in his pockets. "D'you fancy me?" Then his natural shyness overcame him and he blushed. She was looking at him the way you puzzle over a crossword clue.

"Hugh," she said thoughtfully.

He moved closer, until he was just a breath away. He was slightly taller than Natasha, so she looked up into his face. She was beautiful, deadly beautiful. For two long seconds their lips met. Hugh felt a sort of electric crackle that ran the whole length of his body. He took a step back and put his hand to his heart. Kind of … scary. But totally amazing. Natasha was still staring at him in the same blank way.

"Of course," he said irritably, "you don't understand any of this, do you?"

"Try again."

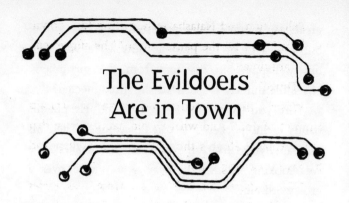

The Evildoers Are in Town

Hugh was finding it more and more difficult to get his thoughts together and stay awake. Slumped on his chair, he stared at Natasha. And Natasha stared at him. She was just standing there, wide awake, seemingly inexhaustible. But what was going on inside? What was she waiting for? Hugh's eyelids were getting heavier and heavier. But he mustn't leave her unmonitored.

"Aren't you sleepy?" he pleaded.

"Hugh," she said, still staring at him.

"Yes, that's right, Hugh. But Hugh's had enough. Hugh's knackered, d'you understand? Hugh wants to sleep, sleep, sleep!"

Exhaustion and Natasha were getting him down.

"Can't you hit the pause button?" he suggested.

"I am timed."

"Timed?"

Was she programmed to stay active for a certain amount of time? And what would happen once that time expired? Hugh's thoughts started fraying, and he gave up asking questions.

"The director of the zoo's on the phone," his mother informed him. *"Apparently it's illegal to keep Sumatran dragons in your home."*

Hugh wanted to point out that Bubble was only a bug, but then he remembered his mother wasn't there. He was dozing off.

The noise didn't wake him. A beam of light burst out of the computer and slowly swept over the study. The time allocated for Natasha to succeed in her mission had expired. She'd failed. Alias had come to recover its creature.

The girl-golem stepped aside to dodge the beam. "There are billions of levels," she said loudly.

She knew something Alias didn't. She knew there was reality and Hugh. She didn't flinch before walking through the study door and re-forming on the other side. She was out of reach there.

Meanwhile, Hugh was informing his mother that he was going to marry Natasha.

"I don't think the director of the zoo would agree to that."

Vexed by this piece of news, Hugh opened his eyes again and saw the beam.

"Natasha?"

She had disappeared.

Hugh threw himself at the computer and shook the monitor, shouting, "Give her back to me! Give her back!"

Did he accidentally hit a key? Or was Alias feeling threatened and wanting revenge? The beam of light expanded and the computer made a noise somewhere between a belch and a hiccup.

Suddenly everything went berserk.

The Evildoers flooded into the study. It was as if the computer was spewing up its guts. Hugh screamed and squashed himself against the wall. He barely had time to make out hooked feet, bats' wings, a snarl exposing the teeth of a vampire, fur, claws, fangs, horns, tails, a whole carnival of monsters (real and imaginary), a fashion parade of nightmares brandishing forks and flares. The mob passed in front of him in silence and walked through the door into the sitting room.

Although the Evildoers seemed to have no substance, Natasha stepped aside to let them pass. Did she feel threatened? As she backed away, she fired. *Peowww! Peowww!* The beam from her eraser-laser went straight through the holograms. No traces. But Natasha had forgotten the real danger: the water from the goldfish bowl. As soon as she trod on the soaking wet carpet, she started crackling. Identifying the threat, she tried to step back.

But it was too late.

A minute later, Alias posted its report on the screen:

Golem Natasha
size: to scale
mobility: good
vision: good
feeling: good
materialization: good
defence: good
invincible armour: inoperative
number of lives remaining: 2

"Oh no!" whispered Hugh, heartbroken. "Two lives!"

Two lives left to love each other. Two lives left for Natasha to understand what life was all about.

Dusk was falling over the Moreland Estate. Big B Stores would be closing in a minute. Aisha was in a hurry. Her mum had just realized they were out of wine. Her dad would be in a bad mood, and when her dad was in a bad mood he lashed out at everybody. She looked up at the stormy sky. The wind was chasing fat, low-lying clouds. It was going to rain soon. She started running, tossing her head to make the beads in her cane-rows clink together.

Aisha had come a long way since that evening when she'd been scared by the strange electric smoke dancing in front of Majid's door. She wasn't so easily frightened any more. In any case, they'd said on TV that farting goo made you hallucinate. That's what it was – she'd been hallucinating and so had Majid. It was all down to FG.

A few metres down the road, Miloud and Rachid were coming out of the doctor's surgery. They'd wasted a whole hour hanging about in the waiting room. Miloud had come this close to smashing the receptionist's face in.

"So there's nothing wrong with you, after all," said Rachid dryly.

"Didn't you hear the doctor? Said I was in shock, innit."

"In shock, yeah, right. He didn't even give you any pills."

They were both jittery. News of the mishap at the BIT Arena had spread and everybody kept winding them up. Rachid kicked the wing mirror of a parked car, shattering the glass. That felt better.

"Do you see what I see?" Miloud suddenly exclaimed. "I like it!"

Aisha was hurrying along.

"Hey, little wifey, where ya runnin'?" leered Miloud, grabbing her as she tried to slip past.

The little Malian girl knew that in situations like this you had to shout very loudly. "Let go!" she cried. "Anyway, I know you. You're Samir's cousin!"

"Well, since we know each other, how about a kiss?" Miloud sniggered.

Rachid watched without getting involved. The

left side of his mouth twitched. Miloud had pinned Aisha and was groping her. The cousins wanted to have their wicked way, and things were looking nasty.

Just then a silent mob came out of the gloom. The Evildoers! A stampede of lecherous beasts, a horde of monsters with twisted faces. When they brushed past Rachid, the shock sent him reeling back against the bonnet of a nearby car. Faced with this infernal vision, Miloud fell to his knees and started crawling away. Aisha thanked God (and the Devil too, to be on the safe side) for freeing her, and went on her way to Big B Stores.

Bernard Martin-Webber had just finished work. He'd fired a heavily pregnant cashier on a trumped-up charge of professional misconduct and was pleased with the way his day had gone. He looked at his watch: 7.47 p.m. He'd got time for a pre-dinner drink with his mistress. Otherwise she'd guzzle the whole bottle of whisky he'd given her on her own. Ever since the BIT Arena fiasco, BMW had been feeling more at odds with the human race than ever.

When he reached his car, he found the wing mirror smashed. Bring back the death penalty, he thought furiously. He got in, started the engine and then, to calm his nerves, put his foot down hard on the accelerator. And again. And again. As he rounded a bend, his tyres screeched and a nightmare vision rose up before him. The Evildoers were sensibly using the zebra crossing, but BMW wasn't expecting a mob of black, yellow and red monsters. Even some blue ones. A riff-raff of fur and feathers, beaks and claws. One of them squashed its steaming face through the windscreen and BMW turned the wheel sharply to get rid of it. As he did so, he collided with a load of dustbins outside a block of flats before hitting the building itself.

"The death penalty," he whispered just before he passed out.

But the Evildoers were already far away and nobody could stop them.

Ten o'clock. The more he thought about it, the more Eddie felt he'd been taken for a ride. Things had got off to a promising start. From his van he'd managed to intercept Albert's call to Granter's mobile. He'd set up the ambush in the bar. He'd got Albert and Granter just where he wanted them. Without that chick, it would have gone like clockwork. Nadia Martin, that so-called teacher. Just who was she working for?

"Hey, come off it," came a voice from the back of the van. "We're not going to park right under her window. She's dangerous, this babe."

Eddie glanced at his new colleague in the rear-view mirror. He looked pretty rough with make-up splotched around his eyes and his beard growing back. Neither of them had had time to change properly. Leather jacket, fishnet tights and a gun. What a sight.

"Right now, I'm not fussed about the details," was Eddie's deadpan reply. "B Corp wants results. They didn't say anything about wanting the girl alive."

The traffic lights turned red and Eddie braked. Even a hired killer obeys the Highway Code. He took the opportunity to pick his nose. Suddenly he froze, a finger up his nostril, eyes popping out of his head.

The Evildoers were crossing the road. Which

was exactly what they should have been doing, because the light was green for them.

"What the hell's that?" roared Eddie's badly made-up companion.

It was a motley, hairy-looking crew, some with bare breasts and claws for hands, a mob of monsters sticking their tongues out till they touched the ground, a gang of obscene creepy-crawlies, climbing on the backs of other creepy-crawlies... Eddie whipped out his gun, leant out of the window and fired. The creatures were streaming busily from one pavement to the other. He lined them up like targets at the fair, but the bullets whistled harmlessly through the holograms. Then they turned down the next street and the nightmare vision disappeared as quickly as it had appeared.

"What was that?" his colleague roared again.

Eddie sat without moving, his head in his hands. "Did you see what I saw?" he asked eventually.

"What on earth was it?"

"The Evildoers."

He'd thought it over and he was sure. The creatures he'd just seen were straight out of Golem, the game invented by Albert. He recognized specific monsters, like the frog with the giraffe's neck, the snake with feet and the giggling Cyclops. Albert must have programmed these things to step outside the game. It didn't make any sense, but the Evildoers were there all right, haunting Moreland Town. Did B Corp know about this? Eddie fished a BIT mobile phone out of his pocket.

"Did you see what I saw?" He wanted to be absolutely sure.

"Yes, but—"

Eddie signalled to him to shut it. He'd got through to Orwell's direct line, Mr William's flunkey. He had to warn him.

"Hello, Mr Orwell? It's Eddie here."

It was 11.21 p.m. The caretaker of Hummingbird Tower peered up at the sky. A fat drop of rain plopped onto his cheek. He could smell the dampness in the wind. The clouds were about to burst.

"OK, hurry up now!" he ordered his dog.

Brutus went over to his favourite bollard and sniffed it.

"Are you going to take a leak, or what?" his master scolded.

Suddenly the wolfhound bared his teeth and started growling.

"Great, you're going nuts again," grumbled the caretaker. For a while now his dog had been scared for no reason, as if he was sniffing out invisible enemies. "Have you finished—" He broke off in mid-sentence.

The Evildoers were there. Zigzagging between Hummingbird Tower and Flamingo Block, panicked by the first drops of rain, but as silently grotesque and businesslike as ever.

Brutus started barking hysterically. The caretaker's legs gave way, and he collapsed onto the bollard.

It was bucketing down as, one after another, the Evildoers exploded into a million sparks.

WHAT do the Evildoers want?

CAN Nadia and Albert foil B Corp's plans?

WILL Mr William stop at nothing to win back Majid's computer — and WHAT does he want it for anyway?

Find out in the next episode of Golem:
Mr William

Turn the page to read Chapter 1...

Class Progress Meeting

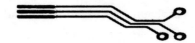

For tiny Mrs Cure – Andrea by first name and maths teacher by job – a class progress meeting was an important event. It was where the futures of the "children", as she insisted on calling them (even when they wore size 13 trainers and had a criminal record), got decided.

Which was why Andrea Cure had been the first to arrive in the staffroom for 8D's progress meeting. She was bent over her register, analysing its contents. Sebastian had scored the highest term average. But her top student had underperformed recently and sometimes seemed distracted in class. Maybe his parents were having a bad time. Or was there a new little brother or sister in the picture? Mrs Cure doodled a question mark. She ran her biro up and down the list in search of the second highest mark, and drew a line under Samir Ben Azet. Who'd have thought it? He might have an attitude problem, but Samir also had real potential. Mrs Cure put an exclamation mark in the margin. She wanted to understand her students. As she reminded the head, Mr Moore, at least twenty times a year, it was important to know about their track record and family background. There was an explanation for everything, even the most alarming behaviour.

The sound of whispering in the corridor alerted her to the arrival of 8D's class representatives. "Come in, children!" she called.

"'Lo, Mrs Cure," mumbled Sebastian and Nouria, before shuffling over to their seats. They looked exhausted as they sat down next to each other, eyes to the floor.

"Is everything all right?" asked Mrs Cure.

Sebastian looked up blankly. Nouria had just told him what Aisha had seen near the Moreland Estate the previous evening. It took a good ten seconds for his teacher's question to sink in.

"Fine," he said at last.

Mrs Cure added another question mark beside his name, increasingly convinced his parents were going through a divorce.

Miss Berry, the history and geography teacher, walked in at this point, and turned bright red on seeing her colleague. "Am I late?"

"No, not at all. I'm early," Mrs Cure said reassuringly. But she couldn't help shaking her head. Poor Miss Berry! How could they get her to smarten herself up? She wasn't exactly ugly, but she slouched and let her hair flop over her face. Not like Nadia Martin, the stylish science teacher who was always sassily dressed.

No sooner had this thought crossed her mind, than in walked Nadia. Mrs Cure stifled a gasp. She looked like she'd just tumbled out of bed. At quarter past five in the afternoon. Her hair was all over the place, her blouse was buttoned up wrong and her mascara had got smudged, giving her a couple of black eyes.

Nadia put a hand to her heaving chest. "Phew! I weally wan!" And with no further explanation, she collapsed onto a chair and put her head in her hands.

Mrs Cure ventured two guesses. One: Nadia had been out partying with her friends and, since she didn't teach on Tuesdays, she'd had a very long lie-in. Such behaviour wasn't entirely appropriate for a teacher, but it was excusable at her age. Two: Nadia had argued with her boyfriend and had been at the sleeping pills. A romantic at heart, Mrs Cure was inclined to believe the second and felt sorry for the pretty teacher who'd just been jilted. But Nadia, who was miles away, started laughing softly to herself. And staring into space. She was picturing Albert as she'd left him half an hour ago in their hotel room. Stark naked. Tanned, buff, fit, the cat that'd got the cream. She let out a sigh that sounded far from heartbroken.

Madame Dupond, the French teacher, turned up next.

"Afternoon all," she said in the rushed tone of voice she used when there was a lot to get through. "Is everybody here?" She frowned, already in a bad mood, and glanced at the clock. She had two small children and was steering a tricky course between earache and chickenpox. "Shall we get started?"

"Er, well," objected Mrs Cure, "we should really make sure that Mr Mu— Ah, here he is…"

Mrs Cure couldn't even bring herself to say hello to Hugh. She just gawped. After several sleepless nights, 8D's English teacher had finally nodded off with his head on the keyboard. He looked worse than exhausted. He was totally run-down. Bloodshot eyes, unruly hair, feverish cracked lips. Mrs Cure knew he'd been off work sick. Was he depressed? He appeared to be on another planet. Or on tranquillizers.

"Right, are we ready?" asked Madame Dupond, interrupting Mrs Cure's train of thought. "Let's start with…" – she smiled at 8D's male class representative – "congratulations, Sebastian!"

"Ah, Sebastian!" exclaimed Hugh, as if he'd only just realized his student was there. "What've you done with Joke? Is he still in the basements?"

Sebastian glanced anxiously at the assembled faces. Was Hugh going to talk about the electric ectoplasm in front of everybody? "Nooo," he replied. "We've put him in the old quarry."

"You can talk about what you've got to move and where later on," cut in Madame Dupond impatiently. "Right, Sebastian, we're satisfied you're ready for Year 9, and well done again. Samir Ben Azet?"

Nadia twitched and seemed to shake herself out of her dream world. "Ah, yes, Thamir!"

It was because of Samir that her life had been turned upside down.

"How did Samir get hold of a BIT mobile phone from B Corp?" she asked out loud.

Hugh's eyes nearly popped out of his head. "B Corp? B Corp must be destroyed," he chanted in a robotic voice.

"That's what Albert thinks," said Nadia.

"You know Albert?"

"Of course I do. I've shared a be— I mean, had dinner with him wecently!" Nadia turned bright red. If she didn't watch out, she'd put her foot in it.

"We *are* here for the progress meeting, aren't we?" asked Miss Berry, always quick to assume she'd got the wrong time or the wrong day or the wrong meeting.

"Of course we are," said Madame Dupond, trying to pick up the pace. "Right, Ben Azet. Are we satisfied he's ready for Year 9? Clearly, there have been a few discipline problems."

"But it's not his fault," Sebastian objected. "He's got to look after his sister, Lulu, who's sick, and his parents drink…"

"Gracious me," whispered Mrs Cure, scribbling *alcoholic parents* in her register.

"And on top of that he's got to make sure Joke gets fed properly," added Sebastian, looking to Hugh for back-up.

"Is that his little brother?" guessed Miss Berry.

Sebastian pictured the giant white monster hiding in the quarry. "Not … exactly," he muttered, hoping Hugh would come to his rescue.

"Not at all," the young teacher corrected him. "Joke is a golem." He looked at everybody sitting around the table. "You *do* all know what a golem is, don't you?" he asked, starting to lose his temper.

There was a thoughtful silence. Mrs Cure wondered if Mr Mullins wouldn't perhaps benefit from extending his sick leave.